"So why the sudden change of role—and the sudden change of outfit?"

"I know. It's awful, isn't it?" Hollie whispered, her stricken gaze glancing down at the clashing colors of red and green of the elf costume.

"I don't know if that's the word I would have chosen," he answered carefully. "I think it suits you, if you want the truth."

"Seriously?" She looked surprised and then shyly delighted.

And wasn't it strange how her obvious self-consciousness was playing sudden havoc with Maximo's senses? The way she was biting her bottom lip was drawing his attention to the cushion of pink flesh that curved so sweetly into a shy smile. Her mouth suddenly looked very inviting. And extremely kissable.

Sharon Kendrick once won a national writing competition by describing her ideal date: being flown to an exotic island by a gorgeous and powerful man. Little did she realize that she'd just wandered into her dream job! Today she writes for Harlequin, and her books feature often stubborn but always *to-die-for* heroes and the women who bring them to their knees. She believes that the best books are those you never want to end. Just like life...

Books by Sharon Kendrick

Harlequin Presents

The Italian's Christmas Housekeeper
Cinderella in the Sicilian's World
The Sheikh's Royal Announcement

Conveniently Wed!

His Contract Christmas Bride

Secret Heirs of Billionaires

The Sheikh's Secret Baby

The Legendary Argentinian Billionaires

Bought Bride for the Argentinian
The Argentinian's Baby of Scandal

Visit the Author Profile page
at Harlequin.com for more titles.

Sharon Kendrick

CINDERELLA'S
CHRISTMAS SECRET

HARLEQUIN
PRESENTS

HARLEQUIN®
PRESENTS®

Recycling programs
for this product may
not exist in your area.

ISBN-13: 978-1-335-14905-3

Cinderella's Christmas Secret

Copyright © 2020 by Sharon Kendrick

This edition published by arrangement with Harlequin Books S.A.

For questions and comments about the quality of this book,
please contact us at CustomerService@Harlequin.com.

Harlequin Enterprises ULC
22 Adelaide St. West, 40th Floor
Toronto, Ontario M5H 4E3, Canada
www.Harlequin.com

Printed in U.S.A.

CINDERELLA'S CHRISTMAS SECRET

In memory of my dearest friend,
Mandy "Gregoire" Morris, who was clever,
cultured, kind and possessed a wicked sense of
humour—qualities that live on in her four amazing
children, Simon, Katy, Robin & Guy.

CHAPTER ONE

'I CAN'T...' HOLLIE'S words came out as a strangled squeak as she held the dress up.

It was very Christmassy. In fact, it *screamed* Christmas—and not in a good way. Short, bright and very green, it gleamed beneath the garish lights of the hotel where the party was being held. She tried again. 'I can't possibly wear this, Janette.'

Her boss's perfectly plucked brows were elevated. 'Why not?'

'Because it's...' Hollie hesitated. Normally, she was the most accommodating of employees. She was a peacemaker. A facilitator. She worked very hard and did what was asked of her, but surely there was a limit. 'A little on the small side...'

But her boss wasn't interested in her objections. In fact, she was even more self-absorbed than usual and had been in a particularly vile mood since her fingernail had chipped that morning and subsequently snagged one of her super-fine stockings.

'Someone of your age can get away with wearing something as daring as that,' Janette clipped out as she adjusted a low-hanging bunch of mistletoe. 'You might find it suits you, Hollie—it'll certainly make a change from your usual wardrobe choices.'

'But—'

'No buts,' continued her boss smoothly. 'We're sponsoring this party, just in case you'd forgotten. And since one of the waitresses is a no-show and with so many VIPs coming, we can't possibly be short-staffed. All you have to do is to turn up dressed as an elf for a couple of hours and hand out a few canapés. Why, if I were a few years younger I would have worn the outfit myself! Especially as Maximo Diaz has agreed to come.' She flashed a veneer-capped smile. 'Potentially the most valuable client we've ever had. Mr Big. Mr Limitless Bank Account. And if his hotel purchase goes through before Christmas, you're looking at a big fat bonus. Surely you haven't forgotten that, have you?'

Hollie shook her head. No, of course she hadn't. How could she have forgotten Maximo Diaz and all the fuss which surrounded him whenever he made an appearance in the small Devon town where she'd moved after her life's savings had become someone else's pocket money? How could *anyone* ever forget a man who resembled a dark, avenging angel who had tumbled to earth in a custom-made suit? A man who made her heart race with uncomfortable excitement whenever he caught her in the hard, black spotlight of his gaze so that she felt like a butterfly pinned to a piece of card.

She swallowed. She guessed every woman felt that way about him. She'd seen the way he was watched by every female who happened to be in the vicinity, whenever he walked into the estate agency where Hollie worked. She'd noticed the way their eyes were drawn—reluctantly or otherwise—to the powerful muscularity of his body and the glow of his olive-dark skin. He was a man who seemed to have taken up stubborn residence in her imagination. A man who symbolised a simmering sexuality and virility which scared her and excited her in equal measure—and no matter how hard she tried, she found it impossible to remain neutral to him.

Not that she would have made very much of a mark on *his* radar. Powerful Spanish billionaires tended not to take much notice of nondescript women who beavered away quietly in the background of large offices. Occasionally she'd made him a cup of coffee, accompanied by one of the home-made biscuits she sometimes brought to the office, if her boss wasn't on one of her rigid diets. She remembered him absently taking a bite from a piece of featherlight shortbread and then looking at it in surprise, as if the taste of something sweet was something he wasn't used to. He probably wasn't. Because 'sweet' wasn't really a word you associated with the rugged tycoon. Hard and dark were words which sprang more readily to mind.

But she shouldn't be thinking about Maximo Diaz—not when Janette was still fixing her with that expectant stare, and automatically Hollie smiled back.

'Of course I haven't forgotten Señor Diaz,' she said. 'He's a very important client.'

'Yes, he is. Which is why all the local bigwigs and politicians are so eager to meet him,' Janette said eagerly. 'He's going to have a big impact on this area, Hollie. Especially if he turns the old castle into a hotel like it was before, back in the day. It means we won't have to use this eyesore of a place any more for our official functions—and not before time.'

'Yes, I do realise that.'

'So you'll do it?'

Hollie nodded. It seemed she didn't have a choice and therefore she would accept the situation gracefully. Wasn't that one of life's most important lessons? 'Yes, Janette, I'll do it.'

'Excellent. Run along and get changed. I've popped in a pair of my own shoes—I think we're the same size. You'll never fit into the other ones. Oh, and wear your hair down for once, will you? I don't know why you always insist on hiding away your best feature!'

Tucking the outfit under her arm, Hollie slipped

from the room, dodging gaudy streamers along the way, trying to concentrate on the evening ahead rather than her boss's rather overbearing manner. Despite being a whole two months until the holidays, the hotel was decked out with yuletide sparkle, which didn't quite manage to disguise the ugly fittings which had seen better days. Yet she wasn't going to complain about the fact that the festival seemed to come earlier every year, because Christmas was a welcome break in the normal routine. A time for candles and carols and twinkling lights. For pine-scented trees and bells and snow. She might not have any family of her own to celebrate with but somehow that didn't matter. It was a time when strangers talked to one another and it brought with it the indefinable sense of hope that, somehow, things were going to get better—and Hollie loved that feeling.

Fluorescent lights lit the way to a gloomy subterranean cloakroom, which was a bit like descending into hell, but Hollie remained determinedly positive as she shook out the fur-trimmed green dress, the red and white striped tights and Janette's scarlet stilettos, which were scarily high.

Peeling off her shirt dress, flesh-coloured tights and sensible court shoes, she stood shivering in her underwear as she struggled into her elf costume. But by the time she had managed to zip it up, she realised her reservations had been well founded because the person who stared back at her from the mirror was...

Unrecognisable.

She blinked, finding it hard to reconcile this new image of herself—and not just because she was wearing what amounted to fancy dress. The no-show waitress must have been much shorter, because the hem of fake white fur swung to barely mid-thigh—a super-short length, which was exaggerated by Janette's skyscraper heels. The other waitress must have been slimmer too, because the green velvet was clinging to every pore of Hollie's body, like honey on the back of a teaspoon. The rich material moulded itself to her breasts and hugged her waist in a style which was as far from her usual choice of outfit as it was possible to imagine.

She looked...

She cleared her throat, hating the sudden nerves and fear which slammed through her body and made her heart race like a train. She looked like a stranger, that was for sure. The way her mother used to look when she was expecting a visit from her father. As if tight clothes could mask a basic incompatibility—as if adornment were the only thing a woman needed to make a man love her. And it hadn't worked, had it? She remembered the bitterness which used to distort her mother's features after she had slammed the door in his wake.

'You can never make a man love you, Hollie, because men aren't capable of love!'

It was a lesson she'd never forgotten—her mum had made sure of that—but not one she particularly wanted to remember, especially now. She wished she could strip off these stupid clothes and the too-high heels. Skip the party and go home to her rented cottage. She could study that new cake recipe she was planning to try out on the weekend and dream about the time when she could finally open her own business and be independent at last. One more year of frugality and she should have amassed the funds she needed. Only this time she would be sure to go it alone, in a part of the world which she found manageable. A picturesque little Devon town called Trescombe—not some big, anonymous city like London, where it was all too easy for a person like her to slip off the radar and become invisible.

Was it that erosion of her confidence which had led to her not paying attention to what was going on around her—until one day Hollie had discovered that nearly all the money had gone and her supposedly best friend had ripped her off? It had been a harsh and hurtful lesson, but she had learnt from it. Never again would she put herself in the position of being conned by someone she'd thought of as a friend, and have her trust in human nature eroded yet again.

And wasn't that another reason for making sure

this party was a success? Because Maximo Diaz's purchase of the old castle on top of the big hill outside town had the potential to herald a new golden age in local tourism and Hollie wanted to be part of it. It hadn't been a hotel for years but was crying out for some love and attention. And if the enigmatic Spaniard was an unlikely candidate to play the part of neighbourhood saviour—well, that was what life was like. Sometimes it threw up surprises and you discovered that people didn't always fit into the little boxes you tried to squeeze them into. Just because a man was an impossibly wealthy global superstar, didn't mean he couldn't also be a good man, did it?

Remembering Janette's parting words, Hollie pulled the scrunchy from her hair and shook her head to let her hair tumble down around her shoulders. It was a colour best described as light brown, though some of the bitchier girls at school used to call it 'mousy'. But it was clean and shiny and it streamed abundantly over her breasts, effectively hiding that rather scary glimpse of cleavage.

The final touch was a red and green hat with a bell on the end and the sound of it jangling like a cash register as she crammed it over her head made Hollie smile. One day soon she would open her very own tea shop and, although she wasn't planning on wearing quite such a revealing uniform, tonight's event would be perfect practice for her future career of serving the public. Wobbling a little in her spindly heels, she headed for the door.

Christmas elf?

How hard could it be?

He didn't want to be here.

Despite the fact that he was poised on the brink of a venture guaranteed to net him even more millions, Maximo Diaz was feeling even more detached than usual.

He looked around at a room which, bizarrely, was decorated with thick streamers of glittering tinsel—even though it was still only October. A giant fir dominated one wall and tiny golden and silver lights twinkled in every available corner of the room. Christmas had, it seemed, come ridiculously early to this one-horse town, with its distant glimpses of the sea and the bleak sweeping moorland which lay to the east.

His mouth hardened.

The truth was, he didn't want to be anywhere right now. Not at either of his homes in Madrid or New York and certainly not here in Devon. Because everywhere he went he took himself with him and 'here' was inside his head, listening to clamouring thoughts which would not be silenced. For the first time in his life, he was finding it difficult to switch off and that disturbed him.

In his past there had been troubles. Of course

there had. Everyone had troubles and sometimes he felt as if he'd netted more than his fair share. Bleak, dark events which had come out of nowhere and threatened to blindside him, although in the end they had bounced off him like hailstones on a pavement because he had willed them to. He had schooled himself to cultivate a steely self-control and had always prided himself on his ability to shrug off hardship. To step away from chaos, resilient and untouched, like a phoenix rising from the ashes. But back then youth, hunger and ambition had been on his side, shielding him against hurt and shielding him against pain. He had come to the conclusion that he was one of those lucky few who were immune to hurt. And if that meant people—usually women—were prone to describe him as cold and unfeeling. Well, he could live with that.

Yet who would have thought the death of someone he'd despised could have pierced his heart so ragged? How was that even *possible*? He hadn't seen her in years. Hadn't wanted to—and with good reason. He should have felt anger or injustice or resentment—maybe all three—as he'd said goodbye to the woman who had given birth to him, summoned to her bedside by the nuns who had cared for her during her final days. Yet it hadn't been like that. He shook his head. His reaction had surprised him. And angered him too, because he hadn't wanted to feel that way. As he'd held her papery hand with its dark tracery of veins, he had felt a deep sorrow welling up inside him. He had been overwhelmed by a sense of something lost, which now eluded him for ever.

And he didn't do that kind of emotion. Not now and not ever.

But he had to carry on. To brush off pointless grief and make like it had never happened. What other choice was there for someone who had turned indifference into an art form? He would get over it because he always did. And he would forgive himself for that rare foray into the saccharine world of sentimentality, because that was a place which held no allure for him.

He would continue with his inexorable rise to the top. He would keep on making a fortune from fundamentally changing the infrastructure of different countries. Building roads and building railways and creating a turnover which caused his competitors to shake their heads with frustration and awe. He had added a luxury hotel chain to his portfolio now and was surrounded by the kind of wealth which, strangely and rather disturbingly, had not brought him the satisfaction he'd sought. But it certainly made women's eyes grow wide whenever they stepped over the threshold of one of his homes or slid into the leather-bound luxury of his private jet. And just because he had more money than he would ever need in several lifetimes, didn't mean he wanted to slow down. Because he liked success. He liked it a lot. Not because of the material rewards it reaped, but for the glow of achievement it provided, no matter how fleeting that feeling proved to be. It was as if he was intent on proving himself over and over again, if not to the father and mother who had rejected him, then maybe to himself.

'Can I tempt you with something to eat, Señor Diaz?'

A soft voice broke into Maximo's reverie and, glad to have the dark tangle of his thoughts interrupted, he turned his head to see a woman standing there, a tray of food in her hands. But it wasn't the unappetising fare which caught his attention and held it, as much as her appearance.

Tempt him? She most certainly could.

His narrowed his eyes, because the thought came out of nowhere, especially as she looked faintly ridiculous in her fancy-dress costume. A sudden pulse beat at his temple and he felt the inexplicable drying of his mouth. Ridiculous, yes—but kind of sexy, too. No. Scrub that. *Very* sexy.

For a moment he thought she seemed faintly familiar, but the thought instantly left him because he was finding it difficult not to stare. And difficult to breathe. Who wouldn't when she looked so…*spectacular*? He swallowed as he continued with his silent scrutiny. Rich green velvet emphasised the porcelain paleness of her skin and a band of white fur at her shoulders drew his attention to her creamy flesh—which was unfashionably soft and abundant. Maximo allowed his gaze to move down, distracted by long legs which seemed to go all the way up to her armpits, an illusion no doubt helped by her teetering shoes. Sexy, scarlet shoes—and most men didn't bother denying their reaction to *that* kind of footwear.

Yet, in direct contrast to the provocation of those killer heels, she wore not a scrap of make-up on her milk-pale face and the healthy sway of hair which gleamed beneath the fairy lights made Maximo experience something he hadn't felt in quite a while. A stealthy but insistent tug of desire, which pulsed through his veins like sweet, dark honey.

His mouth twisted self-deprecatingly. Surely the healthy libido which seemed to have deserted him of late hadn't been stirred by something as off-the-wall as a woman in fancy dress? Maybe his sexual appetite had become so jaded that he was being tempted by a little seasonal role play.

'Um…we have a selection of delicious canapés on offer,' she was saying, her words tumbling over themselves, and something about the softness of her voice made his skin prickle with recognition once more. 'We've got pineapple and cheese on sticks and vol-au-vents—or there's mini quiche, if you prefer.'

'Mini quiche?' he echoed sardonically, dropping his gaze to survey something unrecognisable which was stabbed unappetisingly onto the end of a cocktail stick, and maybe she picked up on his tone because when he looked up again, her face had turned very pink.

'I know they're not to everyone's taste—'

His mouth twisted. 'You can say that again.'

'But the tourist board suggested we go with a retro theme,' she defended.

He found himself unexpectedly charmed by her blush, for when was the last time *that* had happened? 'And why would that be, I wonder?'

'Because nostalgia is big, especially at Christmas.' She hesitated, as if establishing whether he really did want to talk to her or whether he was just being polite. 'Isn't that the whole point of it?'

'But it isn't Christmas,' he pointed out. 'Not for weeks.'

'Yes, I know. But the holiday always puts people in a good mood. And everywhere looks better with a few decorations and a Christmas tree.'

'I must beg to differ,' he commented, shooting a disparaging gaze at the glittering fir with its flashing fairy lights, which was nudging the hotel ceiling. He studied the fake presents he could see piled up at the base and couldn't repress a shudder. 'It looks monstrous.'

She hesitated again. 'You sound as if you don't like Christmas?'

'Something of an understatement,' he returned coolly. 'If you want the truth, I loathe it.'

'Oh. Right. Well, that's a shame,' she said and he could see her biting her lip as she struggled to think of a suitably compensatory response. 'In that case, would you like a glass of bubbly? There's plenty over on the bar—I can easily go and fetch you one.'

He could just imagine the quality of wine on offer but something about her worried expression made Maximo bite back the acerbic response which was hovering on his lips. Suddenly he realised it wasn't fair to take his mood out on her. For him, this party was nothing more than a social necessity—an opportunity to meet the local officials who would help facilitate his ambitious plans. It certainly wasn't what he'd call a pleasure, and she was only doing her job, after all.

And then that first faint flicker of recognition crystallised into something more solid, which made him examine her face more closely, because the dark-lashed beauty of her grey eyes had stirred more than a vague memory.

'Don't I know you?' he questioned suddenly.

She wriggled her milky shoulders a little awkwardly. 'You don't exactly *know* me, Signor Diaz,' she said. 'We've met a few times when you've been into the office. I work in the estate agency you're using to purchase the castle. I'm usually—'

'Sitting behind a desk. *Sí, sí*—of course, I remember,' he said, for hadn't she been an oasis of calm during his recent purchase, and as unlike her abrasive and predatory boss as it was possible to be? She'd made him coffee and served him with something delicious to accompany it. But usually her clothes were unremarkable and her thick hair always scraped back in a style so severe, he imagined even a nun might shun it as unflattering. He remembered thinking that if he were planning on moving his business here, she might make the perfect secretary, and perhaps he would have poached her and paid her twice as much as she was currently earning.

He'd had no idea that beneath her drab clothes was a body which was little short of sensational and he was finding it unexpectedly difficult to reconcile these two dramatically different images of the same woman. 'So why the sudden change of role—and the sudden change of outfit?'

'I know. It's awful, isn't it?' she whispered, her stricken gaze glancing down at the clashing colours of red and green.

'I don't know if that's the word I would have chosen,' he answered carefully. 'I think it suits you, if you want the truth.'

'Seriously?' She looked surprised and then shyly delighted.

And wasn't it strange how her obvious self-consciousness was playing sudden havoc with

Maximo's senses? The way she was biting her bottom lip was drawing his attention to the cushion of pink flesh which curved so sweetly into a shy smile. Her mouth suddenly looked very inviting. And extremely kissable. Bizarre. He shook his head, reminding himself that there were plenty of women more suitable as recipients of his desire than an office junior in fancy dress. 'Are you moonlighting?'

'You could say that.'

She lowered her voice again so he had to lean closer to hear her, and as he did he caught the faint drift of her scent and wondered how something so light and delicate could smell so unbelievably provocative. 'The waitress who'd been hired to do this let them down at the last minute,' she confided. 'And I was asked to—'

'Ah! There you are, Maximo! Hiding away in the shadows, like some dashing conquistador!'

A shrill voice crashed into their conversation and Maximo looked up to see Janette James bearing down on them, her body language managing to be both sinuous yet determined at the same time. She wore a look on her face which he'd seen the first time he'd walked into her estate agency and every time since. It was an expression he'd encountered many times during his life, but especially from middle-aged divorcees.

'I do hope Hollie has been looking after you?' she was saying. 'I'm sure she has, judging by the

amount of time she's been standing here.' She fluttered him another predatory smile before turning
to the hapless waitress by his side. 'But there *are*
other people in the room, Hollie dear, tempting as
it must be to monopolise Señor Diaz. People who
are very hungry. So run along, will you? The mayor
keeps glancing in your direction and he looks as if
he could murder a sausage roll.'

Hollie nodded, aware of Maximo Diaz's burning black gaze on her as she moved away and that
the high heels were making her hips sway in a way
she hoped wasn't drawing attention to her bottom.
Finding the mayor waiting, she kept her smile intact
as he popped an entire sausage roll into his mouth,
and thought about what her boss had said. *Had* she
been guilty of monopolising the Spaniard? Maybe
she had. She'd certainly been transfixed by him.
Lulled by the timbre of his richly accented voice,
she had been unable to tear her eyes away from
his darkly beautiful face. But for once it had been
a two-way street, because tonight she sensed that
she had captured his complete attention. Instead
of flicking her his usual dismissive glance, he had
been openly staring at her and talking to her and
listening to her as if her opinion actually *mattered*.

Had she been gaping at him like a stranded fish
in response to that and drinking in all that powerful
mastery instead of 'working the room' as Janette
had told her to? She turned her head and watched

other people moving towards him, as if they too were being magnetised by all that unashamed masculinity.

'Good-looking fellow, isn't he?' observed the mayor wryly, noting the direction of her gaze as he reached for a second sausage roll. 'I've noticed every woman in the room can't seem to stop staring at him.'

Hollie winced. And she had been as guilty as the rest! She had drooled over him like some teenager at a pop concert.

'I guess everyone's interested because he's about to become a local landowner.'

'You think so? Wouldn't have anything to do with the size of his wallet or the fact that he looks like an old-fashioned matinee idol, would it?'

'Of course not,' she said primly, quickly excusing herself to continue her elfish duties with renewed fervour, in an attempt to redeem herself in her boss's eyes. She dispensed the gradually wilting selection left on her tray, topped up glasses and tried to keep busy, but, irritatingly, her thoughts kept flitting back to the man with the black eyes who was currently being monopolised by the local member of parliament. Maximo Diaz had unsettled her and made her feel distinctly disorientated because when he'd looked at her that way, she'd felt…

It was difficult to describe but she'd felt *different*. As if she weren't Hollie Walker at all, but as if another woman had taken over her body. During a brief conversation about the wisdom of serving throwback cocktail snacks, an entirely different narrative had been running through her head. Hadn't she found her gaze straying to the Spaniard's sensual lips, which looked like an invitation to sin, and wondered what it would be like to be kissed by him? Hadn't her curiosity been piqued about how it would feel to be held in the arms of someone who looked so unbelievably strong?

Which was crazy. A man like Maximo Diaz was about as far out of her reach as the cold stars in the heavens. He was an international playboy with girlfriends who featured regularly on the covers of glossy magazines, while she was a twenty-six-year-old virgin. In fact, sometimes Hollie thought she could be defined by all the things she *hadn't* done. Yes, she'd gone to live in London—and just look how *that* had ended—but she'd never been intimate with a man. She'd never lain naked in someone's arms, or shared a giggling breakfast with them next morning, or gone on a mini-break, or been given a sentimental piece of jewellery.

Maybe that was her own fault. She knew people thought she dressed too conservatively for her age, because they'd hinted at it more than once and Janette had come right out and said so on more than one occasion. But they hadn't grown up watching a woman who used sexual allure like a weapon, had they? Who'd painted her face like a courtesan and squeezed her body into clothes bought solely for the intention of showing off her fabulous physique. But it hadn't worked. Her mother had spent years making herself available to a man who didn't want her and, as Hollie had watched her repeat that humiliating spectacle over and over again, she had vowed she was never going to be like that. Women didn't need a man to define them any more and she was going to live her life on *her* terms.

She cleared away empty glasses and plates and the next time she looked, Maximo Diaz was nowhere to be seen and most of the other guests had begun to drift away. Her heart sank. And that was that. She hadn't even seen him go! Feeling curiously deflated, she brushed up the dropped cocktail sticks and pine needles which littered the floor before making her way back to the basement to change, and by the time she'd bagged up her elf costume, the place was almost empty.

Someone had turned off the flashing Christmas tree lights and the hotel seemed deserted as she left by the staff entrance at the back. But as Hollie stepped out into the dark night, she was unprepared for the rain—or rather, the sudden deluge which was tipping from the sky. With no umbrella and a coat which wasn't particularly waterproof, she was quickly soaked through and her windswept progress to the nearby bus stop didn't provide much in the way of shelter. She looked upwards. Why hadn't the council bothered to repair that gaping hole in the roof?

In vain she scanned the horizon for the welcoming light of the bus and was just contemplating digging out her phone to call a taxi—and to hell with the expense—or even braving the elements and walking home, when a large dark car purred soundlessly down the street and came to a gliding halt beside her.

It wasn't a car she recognised. It was sleek and gleaming and obviously very expensive. A car which looked totally out of place in this tiny Devon town, especially as it was being driven by a chauffeur who wore a peaked cap. But Hollie's heart missed a beat as she identified the powerful figure sitting in the back seat.

The electric window slid down and the shiver which rippled down her spine had less to do with the water slowly soaking through her jacket and more to do with the ebony gaze of Maximo Diaz, which was spearing through her like a dark sword. With a crashing heart she registered his thick black hair and the curve of his sensual mouth, which now twisted in what looked like resignation.

'Get in' was all he said.

CHAPTER TWO

'WHERE TO?' MAXIMO demanded as the woman slid her damp and shivering body onto the seat beside him and his chauffeur shut the door on the howling night.

'I was on my way h-home.'

'I'd kind of worked that out for myself,' he said, steeling himself against the strangely seductive stumble of her words. 'Where do you live?'

'Right on the edge of town, towards the moors.' She turned her face towards his in the dim light of the limousine and he could hear the faint deference in her voice. 'It's very kind of you to give me a lift, Señor Diaz.'

'I'm not known for my kindness,' he told her, with impatient candour. 'But you'd have to be pretty hard-hearted to drive past a woman standing alone at a rainy bus stop on a night like this.' He stared at the raindrops which glittered on her pale cheeks and lowered his voice. 'The question is whether you want me to drive you home, or did your mother warn you never to accept lifts from strangers?'

'You're not exactly a stranger, are you?' she answered primly. 'And since you're offering, then I'll accept. Thank you. It's a rotten night and it really is very…nice of you.'

Nice as well as kind? Maximo almost laughed as he leaned forward to tap the glass and the big car moved forward. When was the last time he'd been described in such glowing terms? The nurses who had cared for his mother in her final days would certainly never have subscribed to such a favourable opinion, but their views on the world had been as black and white as the habits they wore. Nice sons did not neglect their dying mother, nor remain dry-eyed as she shuddered out her last breath.

'Anyway, you can call me Maximo. And put on your seat belt,' he ordered, dragging his thoughts back from the painful past to the woman still shivering beside him.

'I'm trying.'

Waving away her fumbling fingers, he leaned over to slot in her seat belt and as he again caught a drift of scent which was more soap than perfume, he wondered if his behaviour really *was* motivated by a stab of chivalry and nothing more. Because wasn't the truth that tonight he had wanted her—and not in some hypothetical role as his ideal secretarial assistant? Hell, no. Tonight, all the softness and sweetness he'd previously associated with her had collided with a totally unexpected raunchy version, which had planted desire stubbornly in his mind. And he hadn't seemed able to shift it...

Either way, he hadn't intended to take it any further, for what would be the point? She was a small-town woman and he was just...passing through. He didn't do one-night stands. He never had, for all kinds of reasons. They were too messy and had the potential to be complicated, and complicated was something he avoided at all cost. So he had left the hotel and the humdrum party and convinced himself he would quickly forget her—at least until next time he ran into her, if indeed he did. Only by then, she would be back to normal. He wouldn't be dazzled by that very obvious visual stimulant of a short, figure-hugging dress, because she would be back in her drab clothes—barely meriting a second glance as he signed off on his castle purchase. And that would be an end to it. *Adios*. He wasn't intending to stay in this claustrophobic town for a second longer than he needed to. He would sign on the dotted line, put his deal into rapid motion—and nobody would see him for dust.

And then fate had conspired to put her directly in his path—quite literally. No longer a red-and-white-stockinged elf, but a wet and bedraggled woman standing by the roadside. Shivering.

'You're cold,' he observed.

'A bit.'

Commanding his driver in Spanish to increase the heat, he turned to her.

'How's that? Any better?'

'Much better.' She wriggled around in the seat a little. 'It's weird but even the seat feels warm.'

'That's because it's heated.'

'Your car seat has a *heater*?'

'It's hardly at the cutting edge of invention,' he said drily. 'Most new cars do.'

There was silence for a moment.

'I've never owned a car.'

'You're kidding?'

'No.' She shook her head and a few raindrops sprayed over in his direction. 'There's never really been any reason to have one. I used to live in London, where it's impossible to park, and I don't need one here. We need to turn left, please. Just there, past the lamp post.'

Maximo met his driver's eyes in the rear-view mirror and the man gave a barely perceptible nod of comprehension as he started to negotiate the turn. 'So how do you manage without one?'

'Oh, it's easy enough. I walk—when the weather's fine. Or I use my bike. These country roads around here are glorious in the springtime.'

Inadvertently, an image strayed into his mind of a woman on a bicycle, her long shiny hair flowing behind her, while pale flowers sprang in drifts along the hedgerows. He had just allowed this un-characteristically romantic fantasy to incorporate an element of birdsong, when he heard her teeth begin to chatter.

'You're still cold,' he observed.

'Yes. But we're here now. It's the last house—just before the road turns into a mud track,' she was saying, pointing towards a small, darkened house in the distance. 'That's right. Stop just here.'

The car drew to a halt and Maximo saw the chauffeur unclip his seat belt, obviously intending to open the car door, but something compelled him to halt his action with a terse command.

'Permitame...' Maximo murmured, getting out and going to Hollie's side of the car. And even while he was opening the door for her, he was telling himself there was no need to behave like some old-fashioned doorman—not when he'd already played the Good Samaritan and given her a lift home. But somehow he wasn't interested in listening to reason and indeed, he seemed impervious to the hard lash of rain on his face.

'You're getting wet!' she protested.

'I'll survive.'

That look of hesitation was back on her face again. 'Would you...?' She glanced up at the darkened cottage and then back at him as if summoning up a courage she didn't normally call on. 'Would you like to come in, for a cup of coffee? Just as my way of saying thank you? No, that's an absolutely stupid suggestion. I don't know why I made it. Forget it. Forget I said anything.' She shook her head as if embarrassed. 'I'm sure you have somewhere else you need to be.'

He saw the doubt which crossed her face, echoing the ones which were proliferating inside his own head, because this wasn't his style. Not at all. He didn't frequent houses like this and he didn't know women like her. Not any more. He'd left the world of mediocrity behind him a long time ago and had never looked back.

'Actually, there's nowhere I need to be right now and I'd love a cup of coffee. But quickly,' he amended. 'Before both of us get any wetter.'

As he followed her up the narrow path Maximo told himself it wasn't too late to change his mind. He could get his driver to speed out of town, return to his luxury hotel and lose himself in some work—maybe even call that model who'd been texting him for months. The Christmas elf would let herself into her little home, take off her dripping coat—and that would be that. She would be a little disappointed, yes, and even he might experience the briefest of pangs himself, but it would soon pass. He'd never met a woman he would miss if he never saw her again.

Dipping his head to enter the tiny house, he felt the icy temperature hit him. Did she notice his shoulders bunch against the chilly blast as he closed the door behind him?

'I know. It's freezing. I keep the heating off when I'm not here,' she explained, giving a slightly nervous laugh as she switched on a tall lamp.

He didn't need to ask why. She might claim to be nobly conserving energy as everyone was supposed to be doing these days, but he suspected the real reason was a lack of cash. Why else would she be doing more than one job and living in such humble surroundings? He looked around the room, observing the faded rug on the hearth and noticing that the thin curtains she drew across the window didn't quite meet in the middle. Yet the cushions on the sofa looked home-made and a dark red lily in a pot on the table looked almost startling in its simple beauty. And something about the limitations of the room suddenly seemed achingly familiar to him, even though he had grown up in the north-west of Spain and this was England.

He felt the twist of his heart, for it was a long time since he had been anywhere which wasn't five-star. He had embraced luxury for so long that he'd thought those impoverished memories had vanished into the dark abyss of time. Forgotten. For a long time he'd wanted to forget them—no, had *needed* to forget them—but now they came rushing back in an acrid stream.

He remembered the cold and the hunger. The

proud need to survive without letting people know your sweater wasn't thick enough, or that your boots had holes in them. He remembered the slow seep of water making his feet wet and cold. And wasn't that the craziest thing of all—that you sometimes found yourself hungering for the things you no longer had, even if they were bad things? So that when he'd been poor he had craved nothing but wealth and now he had all the money he could ever use, wasn't he guilty of sentimentalising the hardships of the past?

'I'll make you some coffee.'

Her soft words broke into his reverie, her expression criss-crossed with anxiety. Perhaps she'd seen the tension on his face and had interpreted it as disapproval. Maybe that was why she was looking as if she regretted her decision to invite him here. Had he appeared to be *judging* her, when he had no right to judge anyone?

Except maybe himself.

'No,' he said. 'Get yourself dry first. The coffee can wait.'

'But—'

'Just do it,' he reaffirmed harshly.

Unable—or unwilling—to ignore the deep mastery in the Spaniard's voice, Hollie nodded and ran upstairs, her heart pounding with excitement, and started stripping off her sodden clothes, bundling her damp tights into the laundry basket and searching around for something suitable to wear. As her fingertips halted on her best woollen dress, she thought how weird it was to think of Maximo Diaz downstairs, because the only men who ever stepped over the threshold were tradespeople commissioned by her landlord to repair the aging and rather dodgy appliances.

She knew her self-contained behaviour meant she was often regarded as something of an oddity and there were a million reasons she gave to herself and others when asked why she didn't socialise much. She didn't have a lot of spare cash, because she was saving up to start her own business. She hadn't lived here very long, so she didn't know many people. These things were true, but weren't the whole story. The real reason was that her solitary life made her feel safe and protected. It didn't leave her open to pain or deception, or having her life messed up by somebody else.

Yet she had broken the habit of a lifetime and invited Maximo Diaz into her home, hadn't she? A world-famous billionaire financier. She was surprised she'd had the nerve and even more surprised when he'd accepted. And now she had to go down and face him and say…*what*? What on earth did she have in common with the Spanish billionaire?

Yet even though part of her was regretting her impulsiveness, she couldn't deny the slow curl of excitement which was unfurling somewhere low in her stomach. Was it wrong to feel this way about someone she barely knew? She stared in the mirror, her hand automatically reaching for something to tie her hair up, but at the last minute her hand fell back and she left it loose and streaming down her back as she closed her bedroom door behind her.

The creak of the stairs should have warned him she was on her way back down but Maximo didn't appear to have heard her and for a moment Hollie stood immobile on the foot of the stairs. And suddenly it was as though someone had waved a magic wand and filled her ordinary little sitting room with unexpected life and colour, and Maximo Diaz was at the blazing heart of it.

He had lit the fire. Removed his smart suit jacket and put it on the sofa to coax a blaze from the sometimes stubborn little wood-burning stove. Behind the small glass doors, orange flames were licking upwards from the applewood logs and already a blanket of heat was beginning to seep out into the room. Had she thought that a man so rich and so privileged would be unwilling to get his hands dirty? Yes, she had. But it was his stance which surprised her most, for he was sitting back on his heels on the old hearthrug as if he were perfectly comfortable to find himself there. He seemed lost in thought as the flames flickered shadows over his aristocratic profile.

Hollie felt another ripple of excitement whisper-

ing over her skin—a sensation as unsettling as that
low clench of heat unfurling inside her. She knew
she ought to say something but she didn't want to
break the spell. At least, not yet. Because surely
any minute now he would come to his senses. He
would suddenly realise that his driver was waiting
in the car outside and it was time to excuse himself.

Silently, she went into the kitchen and made a
pot of coffee, which she carried back into the sitting room, and when he glanced up and saw her,
something unrecognisable gleamed in the ebony
abyss of his eyes. Something which made her feel
as shivery as before, as if she were standing outside
in the rain again.

Was she imagining it?

Was she imagining the glint of approval as he
ran his narrow-eyed gaze over her?

'Come and sit by the fire,' he said.

His rich voice washed over her like dark silk, as
Hollie acknowledged what sounded like a direct
order. Did he always assume such an air of right-
ful dominance, she wondered—and was it wrong to
find that more than a little exciting? She put the tray
down and sank onto the floor beside him and wondered if she was getting herself into something outside her experience, which a sensible person should
steer clear of. But she was cold, the fire was hot
and the coffee smelt unbearably good. And surely

she wasn't misguided enough to think that Maximo Diaz was actually going to make a pass at her!

'Maybe I should have offered you wine,' she ventured.

'Is that what you want?'

She shook her head. She was already distracted by his proximity—wine was the last thing she needed. 'Good heavens, no,' she said briskly. 'This will be fine. Just so long as it doesn't keep you awake.'

His lips curved into a mocking smile. He looked as if he was about to make a comment, then seemed to change his mind, leaning back against the old armchair behind him and spreading his long legs out in front of him.

For a moment everything in the room became very still—like the preternatural calm which sometimes comes before a storm. The crackle of the fire and the pounding of her heart were the only sounds Hollie could hear and, in the soft light, his eyes looked ebony-dark as he turned his head to study her.

'Have you lived here long?' he questioned.

'Just over a year now. I lived in London before that.'

'Where you didn't have a car.'

She beamed, pleased he'd remembered. 'That's right.'

'So what was the lure of a place like Trescombe?'

Hollie wondered how to answer him. No need to tell him she'd been ripped off. Or that a supposed good friendship had hit the skids as a result. Nobody wanted to hear that kind of downbeat detail and she certainly didn't want to start re-evaluating whether she'd been a hopeless judge of character. And wasn't her new-found motto that she was going to look forward, not back?

'My dream has always been to run a traditional English tea shop,' she told him. 'And when London didn't work out, I heard about an opportunity opening up down here. There's a great site in the town but it won't be available until springtime and until that happens I need regular work so I can save up as much as possible. That's why I'm working for Janette. I'm sorry, I should have asked you before—would you like anything to eat to go with that?'

Reluctantly, Maximo smiled in response to her question. He could sense her eagerness to keep him entertained and knew he ought to cut the visit short rather than get her hopes up, yet he stayed exactly where he was. For the first time in a long time, he felt *comfortable*. Uncharacteristically comfortable. The simply furnished room and warm fire were strangely seductive and so too was her undemanding company. In fact, for someone who was notoriously restless, he might have been able to relax completely—were it not for the undeniable tension which had begun to build in the air between them.

His senses seemed heightened. He could see the thrust of her breasts against the soft jersey of her dress and the pebbled outline of her nipples. He swallowed. It might have been a while since he'd been intimate with a woman but the subliminal message of desire which Little Miss Christmas was sending his way was unmistakable.

And it was driving him crazy.

Was she aware that her eyes grew dark whenever she looked his way, or that she kept trailing the tip of her tongue over her mouth, like an unobserved cat contemplating where its next meal was coming from? And didn't he want to pull her into his arms, to test if those lips tasted as sweet as they looked?

'Why don't you wear your hair down more often?' he said suddenly.

His question seemed to startle her, for she touched her fingers to the silky waves which rippled almost to her waist. 'Because it isn't…' She shrugged. 'I don't know. Practical, I guess.'

'And do you always have to be practical?'

'As much as possible, yes. Life is easier that way,' she asserted, when he continued to look at her. 'You know, more dependable.'

'Really?' he pondered reflectively, the pad of his thumb brushing over the beard-shadowed jut of his jaw—a movement which seemed to fascinate her. 'But surely dependability can get a little boring sometimes. How old are you?'

'Twenty-six,' she said, a little defiantly.

'Don't you ever want to throw caution to the wind and do something unpredictable?'

'I've never really thought about it much, to be honest.'

He noticed that her fingers were trembling, making her coffee cup rattle against the saucer as she quickly put it down on the hearth.

'Well, think about it now,' he said. 'What would you do, for example, if I were to acknowledge the unspoken desire in your eyes and touch you? If I were to brush my fingers against your hair, to discover whether it feels as soft as it looks in the firelight?'

'I can't…' Her words sounded husky and he could see the swallowing movement of her throat. 'I can't imagine you doing something like that.'

'No?' He heard the note of repressed hope in her voice and silently, he answered it, reaching out to imprison a single lock of hair and stroking it between his thumb and forefinger, like a merchant examining a piece of valuable cloth. 'The funny thing is neither can I. But I am. And it does. Like silk, I mean. Rich, dark golden silk.'

'Mr Diaz.'

'I've been thinking about touching you all night long,' he husked unsteadily, skating his palm down over the abundant waves. 'And you like it, don't you? You like me stroking your hair.'

Her shuddered word was barely audible. 'Y-yes.'

For a while he listened to her uneven breathing and felt his own corresponding leap of desire. 'And you know what comes next, don't you?'

She shook her head and gazed at him in silence.

'Yes, you do.'

'Tell me,' she whispered, like a child asking to be told a story.

'I kiss you,' he said, a note of urgency deepening his voice to a growl.

Their eyes met. 'Yes,' she whispered, nodding her head with eager assent. 'Yes, please.'

It was the most innocent yet the most provocative thing he'd ever heard.

And suddenly her hair was a rope and Maximo was using it to guide him towards her waiting lips and he felt his body tense with a sweet and tantalising hunger.

CHAPTER THREE

MAXIMO WAS KISSING HER until she had started to make mewling little sounds of hunger. Until she was moving her body restlessly against him in a gesture of unspoken need.

She should have been nervous about what was about to happen, but fear was the last thing on Hollie's mind as the Spaniard drew away from her, his black eyes blazing with passion in the glow of the firelight.

He laced his fingers through the fall of her hair, and his breath was warm against her lips as he spoke. 'I think it's time we found ourselves somewhere more comfortable, don't you?'

'Yes, please,' she whispered again, and then wondered if she should at least have gone through the motions of pretending to give it more than a moment's consideration.

But that flicker of apprehension fled as soon as he picked her up and carried her upstairs, like the masterful embodiment of all her forbidden dreams. She could hear the powerful beat of her heart and the creak of the wood as he negotiated the narrow staircase.

'Where's your bedroom?' he demanded, once they'd reached the top.

She supposed now wasn't the time to tell him there was only one bedroom—instead she jerked her head in the direction of the nearest door, wishing she had tidied up a bit more. 'In there.'

But as he kicked it open, Maximo didn't seem to notice the cardigan lying on the chair or the pile of cookery books teetering in a haphazard pile on the bedside table. Instead, he set her down and spoke in a voice which suddenly seemed much more accented than before and more than a little unsteady.

'You are wearing far too many clothes,' he growled, skating his fingertips over her trembling body. 'And part of me wishes you'd kept that crazy costume on so I could have had the pleasure of removing it. I've never undressed an elf before.'

Did that mean he didn't like her woollen dress? Probably—it was undoubtedly very staid in comparison, though comparisons were never a good thing, certainly not in her case. But as he peeled it over her head before efficiently disposing of her tights, Hollie suddenly forgot about her insecurities.

'You're shivering,' he observed.

'The upstairs of this cottage is f-freezing.'

'And is that the only reason you're shivering?'

She liked the teasing note in his voice. Was it that which gave her the courage to hook her hand around the back of his head and brush her lips close to his?

'No,' she whispered. 'Not just that, no.'

His soft laugh was tinged with faint triumph as he pulled back the duvet and pushed her down onto the mattress. 'So why don't you warm up the bed for me?' he suggested as he pulled the duvet over her. 'While I get out of these clothes.'

Hollie studied him hungrily as he peeled off his sweater, her mouth drying to dust as his fingers slipped to the button of his trousers. She was grateful that the room was in semi-darkness, which successfully hid the burn of her cheeks as, slowly, he slid the zip down. And she didn't avert her gaze, not once. Even when he kicked off his boxer shorts to reveal the powerful shaft of his erection, though it was the first time she had ever seen a naked man before.

He climbed into bed beside her and when he took her in his arms, she felt so warm and so…safe— that she buried her head in his shoulder, overcome by a sudden emotion she couldn't put a name to.

'*Mi belleza…*' he breathed, exploring her trembling flesh with his fingers until she felt as if she were melting, and then unclipping her bra so that her large breasts came tumbling out. And when he put his mouth to her puckered nipple and sucked,

Hollie felt as if she were going to dissolve with pleasure.

How could it be that she wasn't feeling the slightest bit shy? Even though she was wearing nothing but a pair of panties, which were growing damper by the second as she clung to him as if her life depended on it. Because that was what it felt like. As if she hadn't known what it was to be properly alive before Maximo Diaz kissed her. As if she'd die if she didn't get more of him. More of *this*…this fierce flame of desire which was arrowing through her body and setting her on fire, making her feel as if she were on the verge of hurtling towards some place of unimaginable bliss.

'Maximo,' she breathed, her voice sounding slurred and nothing like her voice at all. 'That is so…so *incredible*.'

His dark head lifted its attention from her breast and his eyes grew smoky as he moved up the bed to kiss her again, his tongue nudging inside her parted lips. And Hollie let her tongue fence with his, loving this brand-new intimacy as her breasts pressed eagerly against his bare chest, as if her button-hard nipples were trying to communicate some unspoken need to him. And instantly he answered it, his hand reaching down to run his fingertip over the damp gusset of her panties. She quivered as he brushed against her swollen bud through the sodden material and felt the whisper of his words on her lip.

'And so are you.' He shook his head and swallowed. 'I never imagined you'd be so…'

'So, what?' she questioned breathlessly.

He seemed to recover some of his poise, tugging at the elasticated edge of her plain panties. 'Well, you're a little overdressed, for one thing.'

'Am I?'

'Mmm…' For a moment he grazed another teasing fingertip over her damp panties, which made her squirm with delight and frustration, before sliding them off and allowing them to join the tangle of other clothes which were scattered over the floor of her small bedroom. 'But you are also hot. Surprisingly hot. Like my every fantasy brought to life. Who knew?'

'So are you,' she whispered boldly, splaying her fingers over his bare chest and thinking how rich his olive skin looked in the soft lamplight. Tentatively she rubbed at one of *his* nipples, silently enjoying his corresponding shudder of pleasure which gave her the confidence to return the compliment. 'You are my every fantasy, too.'

For a moment he grew still, then drew his head away from hers. His black eyes were narrowed but there was no mistaking the sudden warning which glinted from their ebony depths. 'But fantasies aren't real,' he said silkily. 'We both know that, don't we?'

'No, of course they're not. Absolutely they're

not.' Eager to convey her agreement, Hollie nodded, instinctively knowing what he wanted, or, more importantly, what he *didn't* want. He didn't want her reading too much into this and falling for him and, to be honest, that was the last thing she wanted either. She didn't know much about what made men tick but she'd recognised from the get-go that Maximo Diaz was the last person to hitch her star to. Yes, she'd had a crush on him since the first time they'd met and, yes, that feeling had just grown and grown—but she certainly wasn't alone in feeling that way. That she now found herself naked in bed with him wasn't something she'd imagined would happen, not in her wildest dreams. That it had happened in a way which seemed completely natural made her feel comfortable with her own body for the first time in her life and she was grateful to him for that. So why should she deny herself the inevitable outcome of them being here like this?

Why *should* she?

Always, she'd stuck rigidly to the path of convention, because life had felt safer that way. But nothing was ever completely safe and Maximo had been right. For once she wanted to dabble with impulsiveness instead of dependability. She'd never been in love—never wanted to be in love, for that matter—because she'd witnessed the fallout which could result from investing in such an unreliable emotion. She'd never had a boyfriend who had lasted longer than a month and she'd never been turned on enough to get any further than accepting a couple of mechanical fumbles, which had turned her stomach and made her call an instant halt to them.

She'd thought she was one of those women who just didn't feel physical desire. The kind of woman people used to mock and call frigid. But Maximo Diaz was in the process of demonstrating that there was nothing wrong with her body. Nothing at all. Just so long as she didn't start entertaining any unrealistic expectations of some kind of future with the Spanish tycoon. Because that wasn't just impractical—it was stupid.

She closed her eyes as he sank his lips to hers again and moved his hand between her thighs, and Hollie wrapped her arms tightly around his muscular shoulders as if he were her rock and her anchor. How was it possible to feel this good, with a man's tongue in her mouth and his finger strumming at her bare bud with sweetly accurate intensity? But idle reflection was no longer possible, not when a sudden clench of desire was making her heated body as taut as the string of a newly tuned violin.

'Maximo!' she gasped.

He lifted his head, mockery and passion glinting in his eyes. 'What is it?' he husked.

She wanted to tell him to stop. She wanted to tell him never to stop. But then it was happening. Her body had started clenching around his finger, with swift and perfect spasms, and she was crying out something which sounded as if it had been torn from somewhere deep inside her, as the world splintered into a kaleidoscope of vivid rainbows.

Consciousness receded and then came back again in a slow and sensual comedown. She was dimly aware of him watching her and waiting for her body to grow still. He kissed each tingling nipple in turn and then reached for something he must have put on the locker, which she assumed must be a condom. Because Hollie knew the rules—even if she'd never had to follow them before now—and sex had to be safe.

But his hands seemed to be unsteady as he unpeeled the foil and she watched like a hungry voyeur as he slid the rubber down over his erect shaft. Part of her was wondering why she wasn't experiencing a faint wrench of embarrassment, or some element of misgiving at the reality of what was about to happen. But Hollie felt none of those things. Her current state of being was so dreamy and so… *complete* that she simply opened her arms wide as Maximo came to lie down on top of her, welcoming the warm weight of his body.

He was hard and honed and powerful, yet his skin was silky and warm. She was aware of his rigid hardness pressing against her belly and she could feel her thighs opening for him, as if some inner knowledge was orchestrating her movements, making someone with no experience seem as if she knew exactly what she was doing. He gave a low laugh as he positioned himself over her, his lips brushing over hers as she felt his hard tip seeking entry.

'Do you want me, *mi belleza*?'

'*Sí,*' she answered and this made him smile, but as he thrust inside her the smile faded, his eyes briefly closing before he opened them again.

She could feel the sudden tension in his body as he stared at her with a question furrowing his brow.

'Your first time?' he verified.

She nodded, wondering if she'd imagined the note of disbelief in his voice, the lump in her throat making words impossible, terrified he wouldn't want her now he knew that nobody else ever had.

But in that she was wrong.

Very wrong.

Very deliberately, he changed his position, reaching underneath her to cushion her fleshy buttocks with the palms of his hands and bring her thighs up to his hips, so that their bodies seemed even closer than before. He kissed her long and he kissed her hard and just the feel of his mouth on hers was enough to make her relax into what was happening as her body adjusted around him and his incredible width. He began to move again, each thrust seeming to fill her completely—and the sensation of his flesh inside her flesh, of somehow being at *one* with him, blew her mind as nothing ever had before.

Did she wrap her legs around his waist to make his penetration even deeper, or had he guided her into doing that? Hollie wasn't sure. The only thing she was sure of was that those feelings were building up inside her again, taking her higher and higher towards another incredible peak. And then she reached it. Almost without expecting to, she stumbled over the edge and went into free fall and Hollie screamed out her pleasure—she who had never screamed in her life. As she began to spasm around him, she could feel his body begin to buck with pleasure as he bit out words in fractured Spanish—harsh sounds which seemed to split the night.

His movements seemed to go on and on and never had she been so aware of each and every sensation. She could feel the ragged pull of oxygen into her lungs as she tried to steady her breathing. She could hear the muffled pounding of her heart. There was a fine sheen of sweat on Maximo's shoulders and she could detect a raw and very distinctive masculine scent in the air. And now he was heavy against her—as heavy as her eyelids, which felt as if they had been weighted with lead. A sigh fluttered from her lips as she snuggled into his arms and she must have dozed off. Perhaps he did too, for when she woke it was to the realisation that he was growing hard inside her again and Hollie gave a hungry little yelp of longing. Her arms tightened around him and as she began to writhe against him, she could hear herself making wordless sounds of demand against his skin.

'No.' Cutting short her next wriggle of anticipation with a curt order, he carefully withdrew from her.

She was aware of him rolling away and then, to her horror—he carefully peeled off the condom before getting out of bed. His black hair was ruffled as he stared down at her, his jet eyes unreadable as their gazes clashed.

'Where's the bathroom?'

Startled, Hollie searched her befuddled brain for a coherent response. 'J-just along the corridor. You can't miss it.'

After he'd gone, she just lay there, her thoughts in a muddle. At first it shamed her to think she'd just been intimate with a man who didn't even know the layout of her house, but Hollie quickly remonstrated with herself. She wasn't going to feel *any* kind of shame—otherwise what would be the point? And she certainly wasn't going to start getting squeamish and wonder what he'd done with the condom. In fact, she refused to feel any negativity at all about what had just happened. She'd just had sex with a man she fancied very much and it had been amazing. Women the world over did this sort of thing all the time. She had joined the party at last—she certainly hadn't done anything *wrong*.

Sitting up in bed, she smoothed down the mussed tumble of her hair and then Maximo walked back into the room—or maybe she should say *sauntered*—looking totally comfortable with his own nakedness, in all its olive-dark gloriousness. She half expected him to reach for his clothes and start getting dressed, and she told herself she would be okay with that—because what choice did she have?—but to her astonishment, he climbed right back into bed beside her. And then Hollie experienced a little shiver of self-recrimination. Did she think so little of herself that she'd thought he would be out of there as fast as his legs could carry him?

She turned to face him, waiting for him to take the lead, because what did a woman *do* in a situation like this? She had no idea and no experience. Was she supposed to praise him, or thank him for the most incredible happening of her entire life? Or act all cool, as if it were no big deal? Why didn't some enterprising person write a sexual etiquette book for virgins? she wondered.

He lay down beside her and for a moment she thought he was about to lean over and kiss her again and, oh, how she wished he would. But instead, he pushed away some of the hair which had fallen into her face and let his gaze scan over her like a dark searchlight.

'Your first time,' he said again.

It was half statement and half question. 'That's right,' Hollie replied, swallowing down her sudden nervousness that this was going to turn into some sort of interrogation session and she would come over as a freak. 'Do you mind?'

'Mind?' He seemed to mull this over in his head. 'Why should I mind? You're an adult. You have free will. You came to a decision that you wanted to have sex with me. I'm flattered, of course, and more than a little interested to know why.'

She wondered if he was fishing for compliments. Did he want her to say he was so gorgeous that she hadn't been able to resist him? *And wouldn't that have been the truth?* But Maximo Diaz needed no boost for his ego, not from her. Certainly not when he was lying there, dissecting what had just happened between them with all the cool detachment of a scientist in the lab. 'Does there have to be a reason?'

He shrugged and the ripple of muscle beneath his broad shoulders was more than a little distracting.

'Most women wait—though I guess you've waited quite a long time already—for a long-term relationship in which they can feel comfortable. Something which has a little more depth.' He paused. 'And history.'

It sounded like an accusation. Or a reproach. Was

he somehow *disappointed* that she hadn't made him wait? 'Maybe I'm not most women.'

'No. Maybe you're not. In fact, I would take that as a given. You are certainly very surprising. You confounded my expectations which, believe me, doesn't happen very often.' He gave a short laugh before fixing her with that glittering black gaze again, their bodies still very close, the slick of his sweat-sheened skin sticky against hers. 'So which is the real you, I wonder—the efficient mouse who slaves away behind her desk, or the minxy hostess in fancy dress who wiggles her bottom so provocatively when she walks?'

'It was the shoes which made me walk that way.'

'Ah, so we must blame the shoes, must we?' he questioned gravely.

'I borrowed them,' she explained, when she saw the glint of mockery in his eyes. 'Oh. I see. You're teasing me.'

'Yes, I am teasing you, *mia belleza*,' he said, and his voice suddenly deepened into a velvety note of intent. 'But not for very much longer, because teasing inevitably provokes desire. What I would most like to do to you right now is to kiss you again and then to—'

'Make love?' she put in eagerly, then could have kicked herself for her naivety, which was surely responsible for the sudden tension which had entered his body.

'Well, that is one way of describing what we are about to do, though you need to remember that this has nothing to do with love.' His golden olive features hardened. 'Love is a concept invented by society. As a bribe, or a threat. As a marketing tool used by big businesses. Or as a method of control—a way of regulating women's behaviour.'

Hollie opened her mouth to object to what sounded like pure cynicism, until she realised that she agreed with him. Every single word. Hadn't her own mother carried her supposed 'love' for her father around with her like some dark jewel pressed close to her heart—guarding it and polishing it and making it more important than anything else in her life, including her own daughter?

'What *does* it have to do with, then?' she questioned boldly, because why wouldn't she be bold when she had come this far? When she was naked and glowing with physical satisfaction, even though the turn of the conversation was proving a little too raw for her liking. But then the insistent little clench deep at her core made her realise that she would prefer to stop talking altogether, and start kissing…

Did he read her body language? Was that why he reached out to stroke her face, his thumb whispering to her neck, where it lingered on the frantic little pulse which was beating there? Hollie shivered as he continued with his journey and it seemed to take for ever before he reached her nipple, his eyes not leaving hers as he massaged its diamond hardness, a small smile playing at the edges of his lips as it pebbled beneath his thumb. And she realised he still hadn't answered her question.

'It has to do with sensation. With feeling,' he answered, as if he'd read her mind. 'And this is the best feeling in the world. Wouldn't you agree?'

'Yes.' There was a short silence while she fought and lost the battle to let the subject go. 'But you've felt it before, I suppose? Probably lots of times.'

He didn't deny it. 'Of course. But not for a while.'

She wanted to ask, but Hollie told herself it was none of her business. That his answers might not be what she wanted to hear. And when she didn't say anything—which seemed to surprise him— he moved closer. So close that at the points where their bodies connected, she could feel goosebumps icing her skin.

'So why don't we enjoy what we have? Just for tonight,' he added softly. 'I could send my chauffeur home and we could enjoy a little more uncomplicated pleasure. I could show you many different ways to achieve orgasm. We could explore and enjoy each other's bodies, because yours is…'

Hollie felt a feeling of power as his finger drifted down over her sternum, to lie possessively on the soft flesh of her belly. 'Mine is what?' she questioned breathlessly, as if she had conversations about the nature of desire every day of the week.

'*Esta magnifica.* So soft, so womanly, so full,' he husked, beginning to knead her flesh with his fingers and making her want to moan with delight. 'I want to be inside you again. Deep inside you. As many times as I can. Do you want that, too?'

Of course she did and she nodded eagerly. Who wouldn't want it? But his husky question came with a coded warning. *Just for tonight*, he had emphasised. Which meant she mustn't expect anything more. His words weren't the stuff of dreams or fairy tales, but that didn't mean she had to shoot them down in flames. At least he was being honest with her. At least he wasn't playing games and messing with her head, which meant something to a person who had been brought up to believe that men were nothing but inveterate liars. And now he was reaching down for his discarded trousers and sliding his phone from the pocket to have a rapid conversation in Spanish, presumably with his chauffeur, laughing briefly before hanging up. What was he laughing about? she wondered. But suddenly her slight paranoia was forgotten because he was pulling another condom from his wallet and in that moment Hollie felt properly grown-up for the first time in her life.

She was having sex! The amazing Spaniard had already given her, not one, but two orgasms—and he was planning on giving her some more! Christmas really had come early!

She settled back against the pillows, anticipation

shivering her skin as he began to stroke her, with that look of dark intent on his face which made her melt inside. And then he ruined it all, as he brushed his lips over hers.

'Do you realise,' he mused, his hand reaching comfortably for her breast, 'that I don't even know your name?'

CHAPTER FOUR

HOLLIE'S MOUTH DRIED as she waited. She was trembling. Of course, she was trembling. Who wouldn't be in her situation?

She closed her eyes, uttering some kind of wordless prayer, but when her lids fluttered open, her wish had not been granted. Nothing had changed. She was still staring through the window of her tiny cottage at the dark night outside and the Christmas lights in the window of the house opposite. She was still exactly the same woman she'd been seconds ago.

She swallowed.

Pregnant.

Pregnant with the Spanish tycoon's baby.

Her heart pounding, she knew she couldn't keep putting off the inevitable. She needed to tell Maximo and the longer it went on, the harder it seemed to be.

She was still finding it hard to get her head around what she'd done. After a lifetime of being a virgin, she'd fallen into bed with a man who was practically a stranger. She couldn't have found a more unsuitable man to be her first lover, if she'd tried. An international playboy who had seemed all too eager to put distance between them once their brief encounter was over.

The night had not ended on a particularly good note. She'd hoped he might stay on for a while next morning. She'd thought about making him pancakes for breakfast, with honey or cheese. Or an omelette, maybe—because didn't the Spanish use a lot of eggs in their cooking? Perhaps she'd been secretly hoping to impress him with her undoubted skill at all things cuisine—the way to a man's heart and all that. But no. He had climbed out of bed, all glorious and glowing and naked, when the dawn light had been nothing but a glimmer on the horizon. She must have slipped back into sleep because the next time her eyelids had fluttered open, he had been fully dressed and maybe she should have guessed what was coming from the terse tone of his words.

'I'd better go.'

'Oh. Must you?' Her voice had been little more than a murmur, but afterwards she wondered if she'd sounded a little *needy*.

'I'm afraid I must. I've called my chauffeur to come and pick me up. I have a meeting.'

She remembered thinking it was very early to be having a meeting and then, drugged with satiation and satisfaction, she had fallen into a deep sleep and when she'd woken up, he had gone.

It had taken nearly a week for her to realise Maximo wasn't going to contact her again. He had told her he wouldn't but hadn't there been a stupid glimmer of hope which had taken up stubborn residence in her mind and made her hope he might change his mind? But there had been no phone call. No flowers. No unexpected dropping in at the estate agency to ask whether she might happen to be free for lunch—and of course she would have said yes, because her daily home-made sandwich, which reposed at the bottom of the office fridge, could easily be eaten another day.

But Maximo had done none of these things. The purchase of his castle was now complete and everyone in the town was breathlessly waiting for the refurbishment to begin, when he would turn it into the most talked about hotel in Devon to add to his prestigious group. She assumed that was why he was here today. She'd heard he was having high-powered meetings in the nearby city of Exeter and so, when Janette had left the office to have her nails painted, Hollie had hunted around for the tycoon's telephone number and had sent him a text, asking if she could see him.

His answer hadn't exactly boosted her confidence, or her resolve. It had been blunt and to the point. Some people might even have called it rude.

I'm very busy.

She wished she could have told him to take a running jump, but that was exactly what he would like her to do, she reminded herself bitterly. Her finger had been shaking with rage and she had wasted time correcting several typos as she had furiously tapped out a response.

I'm sure you are, but I need to see you.

She'd been forced to wait for a whole hour before the reluctant reply had come winging back.

I can give you half an hour at six p.m. Where?

That had made her hesitate. Neutral territory would be best. But she couldn't risk any kind of scene, not in a town this small where people would talk. And so even though uncomfortable memories of last time he had visited her cottage wouldn't seem to leave her alone, Hollie forced herself to reply.

Can you come to my cottage? I assume you remember where it is?

And the terse rejoinder.

I'll see you there.

It seemed insane to think about it now, but she'd actually made some biscuits in preparation for his visit, which were currently sitting on her best china plate in the kitchen. She'd told herself it was more to give herself something to do, rather than pacing the floor as she waited for the smooth purr of his limousine. But the insane truth was that she was making shortbread because she knew he liked it.

It was pathetic, really. Did she honestly imagine that the sugary cookie was going to make him smile and tell her everything was going to be okay, and he was fine with the fact that she was carrying his baby after what was only ever supposed to be a one-night stand?

She turned away from the window and glanced around the small sitting room, her gaze coming to rest on the miniature Christmas tree she'd forced herself to decorate, even though she hadn't been feeling remotely festive at the time. Its rainbow lights were pretty and the little baubles she'd crafted herself usually filled her heart with seasonal joy as she dangled them from the pine branches. But she had been so bogged down by a feeling of dread at what she was about to do that not even holiday decorations had been able to lighten her mood.

She heard the sound of a powerful engine and quickly ducked away from the window, not wanting to be seen watching and waiting, like some kind of crazed stalker from a horror film. She drew in a deep breath as she heard the approaching crunch of footsteps and slowly expelled it as the doorbell jangled.

Silently counting to three, Hollie walked calmly towards the door, trying to mentally prepare herself for the sight of Maximo Diaz as it swung open. And even though she had thought about him every single day since their night of passion, Hollie was still unprepared for the visceral impact of seeing him again.

He looked…

Her heart rate, which had already been elevated, now began to pick up into a deafening crescendo as she stared at him.

He looked…incredible.

Dressed entirely in black, he wore jeans and a buttery leather jacket, beneath which was a sweater so soft it could only have been made from cashmere. But that was the only soft thing about him. His body was hard and his face was even harder. Black eyes studied her as coldly as chips of jet and those wickedly sensual lips were set and unsmiling. How weird it was to think of all the pleasures those lips had showered on her while they'd been in bed together, when now they seemed to flatten at the edges with a look of faint disdain. Or was that her imagination?

Hollie knew she had to pull herself together. She couldn't keep catastrophising or trying to get inside his head. She had to act as normally as possible, although that was never going to be easy given what she was about to tell him. How would she have spoken to him if she hadn't had sex with him? How did she used to speak to him when he came into the office, during those easy, uncomplicated days before she'd been stupid enough to allow him to seduce her? With an enormous effort, she fixed a bright smile to her lips, aware of the stupidity of her greeting even as it tumbled from her.

'Good afternoon, Señor Diaz!'

Maximo tried very hard not to react to the instinctive punch to his gut as he studied the woman standing before him. He should be on his guard after her rather embarrassing determination to see him, yet all he could think about was her pale, soft flesh and the thickness of her shiny golden-brown hair as it had tumbled down over her bare breasts. Was that unwanted reaction responsible for his drawled words, which weren't the words he intended? 'Don't you think such formality is a little inappropriate, in view of what happened?'

'Even though you didn't even know my name at the time?' she answered quickly.

Maximo winced. She was right. How had that even *happened*? He still wasn't sure, and looking at her now provided no easy answers. The provocative minx in the towering red heels and thigh-skimming green dress was nothing but a distant memory, for she'd reverted back to her usual sensible look. Her magnificent hair was tied back into a tight bun and her lips were bare. She wore a neat skirt and forgettable sweater, which had obviously not been bought with the intention of emphasising her curves, and her brown leather boots had seen better days. They were obviously old boots which had been carefully polished—and something about that recognition of someone who was 'making do' struck a raw and distant chord deep inside him. She looked unremarkable, yet... He frowned. Wasn't there a glowing inner quality about her, which seemed to transcend her rather drab appearance?

'But I do know your name now,' he said, attempting a placatory smile. 'Hollie.'

'Hollie Walker,' she supplied crisply and then blushed, and that only seemed to emphasise her innocence.

Had he really had sex with her? Taken her virginity in one smooth and delicious thrust? Yes, he had. And it had been amazing. No. That wasn't quite accurate. It had been nothing short of sensational. Turned on and beguiled by those long legs and cascading hair and the startlingly dramatic change in her appearance, Maximo had succumbed to a one-night stand in a way he hadn't done since his teenage years. Her innocence had come as a shock and he still wasn't quite sure why he hadn't extricated himself from the situation as quickly as possible after that first time, doing them both a favour and recognising that someone like him was bad news for a small-town woman like her.

But he hadn't. He had carried on losing himself inside her sweet, tight body for most of the night, over and over again. And when they'd eventually run out of condoms—something which had never happened to him before—he had pleasured her in other ways. He had used his tongue and his fingers and, at one point, an ice cube from the freezer downstairs, he recalled—so that the memory of her shuddered cries of fulfilment had stubbornly lodged themselves in his brain for days afterwards. He'd had difficulty forgetting the way she'd cried out his name and the way her soft thighs had wrapped themselves around his thrusting back. He'd had difficulty concentrating on work too, drifting off into sensual daydreams at the slightest provocation, until he had forced himself to stop thinking about her.

But none of those things addressed his immediate concerns and now a feeling of wariness crept over him as he looked into Hollie Walker's face. Because, why had she asked to see him? Deliberately pushing away the brief cloud of darkness which hovered on the edge of his mind, he met her gaze with a look of polite enquiry.

'So. What can I do for you, Hollie? I meant it when I told you I was busy. There are things I need to get finished before Christmas, which is in a few days' time, as you clearly know.' He forced himself to give a curt nod of acknowledgement in the direction of the smallest tree he had ever seen.

Her mouth was working and her previously glowing complexion had paled. 'There's no easy way to say this. I wish there was.' She clenched her hands into two fists and squeezed them tight until the knuckles grew white. 'I'm pregnant, Maximo,' she husked. 'I'm going to have your baby.'

The world spun and a dull sound inside his head threatened to deafen him. For a minute Maximo thought he must be dreaming, but her trembling body and white face were real enough and told their own story.

For this was no dream. The nightmare had become real.

'You can't be.' His words were icy but the anger growing inside him felt hot and vital and all-consuming. 'We took precautions.'

'Well, obviously those precautions didn't work,' she said. 'Look, I realise this has come as a complete shock to you—'

'But clearly not to you.' He frowned as he did some rapid mental calculations. 'We had sex in—'

'October,' she supplied swiftly, her cheeks flaming. 'Just in case you're muddling me with someone else.'

'There hasn't been anyone else,' he snapped before wondering why on earth he had told her *that*.

Because wouldn't it give her more power than she already had if she realised that every other woman had left him cold since he'd exited her bed, that wet dawn morning? Would she mistakenly start thinking she was special, or different?

'Oh. Right,' she said, looking startled.

His gaze skated over her as it had done with so many women in the past, but for once there was only one place it was focussed on. Not on her hair or lips or the curve of her breasts, but on her abdomen. 'Pregnant,' he repeated, as if affirming what his naked eye could not see.

'Eleven weeks.'

He felt as if he were speaking in a language he didn't really understand. As if he had entered a world which was now defined by dates. 'You certainly took your time telling me.'

She nodded. 'I know. I didn't realise for a while. At first I couldn't believe it, because I thought we were so careful. I made myself do three tests, until eventually I had to accept the evidence of what I found. And you weren't around to tell, Maximo. You were supposed to be coming back to Trescombe. Everyone thought work was going to start on the castle before Christmas—'

'What work?' he demanded.

'Well, you're turning it back into a hotel, aren't you? It's been the talk of the town for months. But you just…disappeared.'

'I have a global business,' he informed her coldly. 'Which seems to have gone into overdrive lately.'

'And was that…?' Her face was screwed up and she seemed to be forcing herself to ask the question. 'Was that the only reason?'

Maximo's mouth hardened. Wasn't it better she knew? Better to trample on her foolish dreams rather than to allow them to flourish unchecked? 'Not the only reason, no. If you must know I thought that creating space between us would ensure you didn't get the wrong idea about what had happened. I didn't want you building castles in the air.'

'You're the one with the interest in castles, Maximo,' she said coldly. 'I told you at the time I was okay with it.'

'Women say all kinds of things they don't mean, Hollie. They say them to save face, or sometimes to convince themselves that they actually believe them.'

She glared at him. 'And you were so certain I'd be a thorn in your side with my unwanted devotion that you didn't want to risk a return visit, is that it? Were you worried I'd believe I was hopelessly in love with you?'

'That was always a possibility.'

'Even though you're proving to be so arrogant and unlikeable?'

He shrugged. 'You were an innocent. A virgin. Sometimes a woman's first experience of sex can warp her judgement, particularly if it was as good as yours was. I'd warned you what kind of man I was but I wasn't sure whether you wanted to believe it. But all that is irrelevant now.'

He realised she was looking at him and the reproach on her flushed face suggested she had been hurt by his condemnatory assessment of their night together. But he wasn't going to tell lies in order to spare her feelings. She needed to know the truth, because surely that would limit the painful repercussions of a situation he had been so determined not to create during his own lifetime. The legacy of his upbringing was bitter enough to taint him for ever and he didn't want to feel trapped. Not ever again.

'I've never wanted marriage or children,' he bit out. 'And while the first is within my power to control, the second is clearly not.'

'But I'm not asking you for anything!' she declared furiously, her fists still clenched and looking as if she would like to use them to punch him. 'I can manage perfectly well on my own.'

He glanced around the small room. At the handknitted blanket on the battered sofa. At tired-looking walls, which even the rainbow glow from the fairy lights on the Christmas tree couldn't quite disguise. He remembered the narrow bed in the cold bedroom upstairs, where he had torn the clothes from his body with the eagerness of a boy who had never had sex before. And the speed with which he had made his escape the following morning, issuing a terse directive to his chauffeur to get him the hell out of there when the car had arrived.

And all he could think was—what had he *done*?

'What, here?' he demanded. 'You think you can bring up this baby here, in a place like this?'

'Of course I can! It may not be grand and I may not have a lot of spare cash, but I will manage. I don't know how, but I will. I'm not deluding myself that it's going to be easy, but I'm not afraid of hard work. It won't hurt me to scrimp and save and go without—but there's one thing my baby will never go short of, and that's love!'

An expression of such fierce protectiveness came over her face, that Maximo found himself unexpectedly humbled by her fervour, until he reminded himself that words were cheap. 'Very admirable,' he drawled.

'I'm not seeking your approval.' Angrily, she shook her head. 'In fact, I don't want anything from you, Maximo Diaz. Because I don't need you! Do you understand?'

But he shook his head, as if she hadn't spoken. 'I am not dishonourable enough to desert you in your time of need, just as long as your expectations don't exceed what I am prepared to offer you,' he bit out, withdrawing his wallet from his inside pocket and extracting a business card. He slapped the card down beside the Christmas tree with more force than he had intended, causing the flimsy baubles to jangle before striding towards the front door, barely able to contain the anger which was simmering up inside him.

He pulled open the door. 'You can telephone my office and they will give you contact details of my lawyer, who will fine-tune all the necessary arrangements,' he concluded icily. 'You will have the necessary funds to employ nannies, chauffeurs, cleaners—whatever it is you think you might need to make your life easier once you have a child. But there is one thing you're never going to get, Hollie—at least, not from me—and that's a father for your baby.'

CHAPTER FIVE

'HOLLIE, ARE YOU even listening to what I'm saying?'

Hollie swallowed. No, of course she wasn't listening—not properly, anyway. She hadn't been fully concentrating on Janette's words, just as she hadn't been concentrating on anything lately. Not the news, nor office views, or even the fact that it was Christmas tomorrow. The only thing which was eating up her mind was the terrible showdown she'd had with Maximo a couple of days ago, when she had told him she was expecting his baby and he had reacted with…

Anger?

Disbelief?

Yes, both those things—and more besides. He had been icy with her, and distant. He had seemed to go out of his way to push her away and to view her with coldly dispassionate eyes. Nobody would ever have guessed they'd been lovers. Although, if you didn't even get to share a whole night with a man—did that actually *count* as being a lover?

That had been bad enough but worse was to follow because when she'd arrived at work the next morning, Janette had asked could she make a cake for Maximo, to celebrate his completion on the purchase of the castle. It had been the last thing on earth Hollie had felt like doing, but what excuse could she possibly use for declining?

I'm terribly sorry, Janette, but I'm pregnant with Maximo's baby and he's being so unreasonable that I'd be tempted to tip a dollop of arsenic into the mix.

No, she had nodded her head submissively, even though her heart had wrenched with bitterness and shame. And as she had beaten the eggs and measured out the sugar, she had been unable to flush the image of Maximo's angry face from her mind and to wonder where they went from here. She still had the business card he'd given her, just before he'd made his arrogant assertion that she should contact his lawyers.

He had cold-bloodedly stated that his money would enable her to employ a whole stable of staff, and had ended the conversation by announcing that he had no intention of being a father to his child. Well, that suited her just fine. Did he really imagine she, or her baby, wanted *anything* to do with a man who hadn't bothered to hide his dismay when she'd told him her momentous news?

But surely the most important thing right now was to hang onto her job, at a time when she had never needed work more badly. Which was why she looked up at her boss and forced a weak smile. 'What were you saying, Janette?' she asked.

'I was congratulating you on your cake, Hollie, which is absolutely lovely—though I have to say that it's not quite up to your *usual* standard.'

Hollie nodded. Of course it wasn't. It was unfortunate that a huge salt tear had plopped onto the finished product at the very last minute and Hollie's subsequent attempts at repair work only seemed to have made it worse.

'I know it's not that good,' she said.

'It can't be helped.' Janette's words were brisk. 'I'm sure he won't notice. It's the thought that counts, and this will make him realise that our agency is always prepared to go the extra mile—just in case he's thinking of buying any more local property in the area. Just make sure you deliver it today, can you, dear?'

'D-deliver it?' Hollie could see from Janette's expression that she hadn't quite managed to hide the horror in her voice. 'You mean deliver the cake? To…to Maximo?'

'To *Señor Diaz*,' Janette corrected, frosting her a severe look. 'Since when did you start using first

names with clients, Hollie? Of course, I mean you!
I thought you'd be delighted to comply after the
way you monopolised him at the party. And who
else is going to do it?'

'But—'

'Most people are very busy this close to Christmas, but at least you haven't got any family. I'd
do it myself except that I have a date through that
new site—Flirty at Fifty. I mean, it sounds almost
too good to be true, but, still…' Janette's steely-
eyed look couldn't quite disguise the unmistakable
glint of hope which lurked in her heavily made-up
eyes. She shrugged. 'Mustn't look a gift horse in
the mouth and all that. Just make sure the cake arrives at the castle this afternoon, will you? There
are a few more papers he needs to sign at the same
time. But you'd better get a move on.' She shot a
quick glance out of the agency's big glass windows.
'I don't like the look of those clouds and they're
forecasting snow over the holidays. Dave can drop
you at the bottom of the lane on the way to his four
o'clock appointment and you can easily walk back.'

Behind her frozen smile, Hollie felt as if she were
in pieces, chewed up by a growing feeling of dread
at the thought of seeing Maximo again. Their last
meeting had been bad enough. The awkwardness
and embarrassment of facing the reluctant father
of her baby was an episode she wasn't eager to repeat. But without having to explain *why* she didn't

want to go—and just imagine Janette's reaction if she did *that*—common sense told her that refusal simply wasn't an option.

Common sense.

How ironic that something she had relied on all her life had deserted her when she needed it most. If she'd been sensible she wouldn't have fallen into bed with him—seduced by a lazy smile and a hard body, and a smooth line in seduction.

She glanced out of the window, where the main street was bustling with last-minute shoppers, and as she looked up at the sky she could see that Janette hadn't been exaggerating. The heavy pewter clouds looked bloated and full and there was a strange saffron light radiating downwards, making the seasonal colours in the shop windows even more vivid than usual.

Christmas trees were laden with baubles and strings of fairy lights created magical grottos. Branches of greenery and berries were swathed in thick, fake snow—but occasionally a flake of the real stuff fluttered down to lie on the glittery pavement. Strings of tinsel sparkled as brightly as the midday sun and jolly figures of Santa were tempting little children to tug on their mother's hand to try to get them to linger.

Hollie's heart slammed against her ribcage.

Little children.

That was what she would have before too long.

A child of her own. First there would be a baby and then the baby would grow into a toddler and then…

But, no. Before she started trying to imagine an unimaginable future, she needed to deal with the present and there was one thing which couldn't be put off any longer. She would deliver the wretched cake to Maximo and get him to sign the papers. She would do both these things in a calm and outwardly relaxed manner, and if he brought up the subject of his lawyer again, she would tell him that these things would probably be better addressed once the seasonal break was over and the dust had settled.

At just after three, Dave's rather beaten-up old car dropped her off at the bottom of the lane and, carefully clutching the cake box, Hollie began to climb the steep hill towards Kastelloes. From here the ancient grey castle looked faintly forbidding as it dominated the green landscape with its turrets and its towers. It hadn't been a hotel for a long time but Hollie's excitement at the thought of it being brought to life again had been somewhat dampened by the dramatic changes in her own fortune.

She tried to imagine bringing a new life into the world. Would she still be able to open her tea shop with a tiny infant in tow—was that going to be possible, despite all the proud protestations she'd made to Maximo? As her reluctant steps carried her closer to the castle, she noticed that the snow was starting to fall more heavily and coating her cheeks with big white blobs.

There was no sign of life as she walked over the drawbridge and past the old gatehouse. No Maximo rushing out to relieve her of her burden as she came to a halt in front of the ancient oak door. If he wasn't in, then he wouldn't be able to sign the papers, would he? And Janette would just have to accept that. But an upwards glance showed a golden light gleaming through one of the mullioned windows, indicating that *someone* was home, and, although her heart was plummeting, Hollie knew she couldn't back out now.

She paid the driver and, after putting the cake box down on the doorstep, pulled the bell and heard a faint ringing from somewhere deep inside the castle. She looked around as she waited, trying to enjoy the vision of the falling snow covering the stone pots and statues with a fine layer of white. But more importantly, it allowed her to look away from the door, because she didn't want Maximo opening it and finding her staring up at him with anxiety written all over her face. She needed to show him she was in control, even if she didn't particularly feel that way.

Her hands were cold and she wished she'd remembered to bring gloves with her. Her coat felt inadequately thin and the breath leaving her mouth was coming out in big, white puffs. She was just beginning to wonder if anyone *was* at home when the door of the castle opened with a creak and she turned to see Maximo standing before her, his powerful frame outlined by its arching wooden frame. Hollie felt her stomach somersault and silently cursed—but what could she do about her instinctive reaction? Despite everything which had happened between them, she obviously hadn't acquired any immunity to him. And no wonder. Dressed in his habitual black, he looked as if he had arrived from another age. As if he were thoroughly at home in this windswept citadel, high on a hill. A conquistador, Janette had once called him and, with all that powerful and brooding darkness he exuded, didn't her boss have a point?

'Hollie,' he said. His rich Spanish accent filtered over her skin like velvet but there was a frown creasing his brow. 'This is a…surprise.'

And obviously an unwelcome one, judging by his acid tone. 'I have some papers for you to sign,' she said, instantly on the defensive, determined to ensure he understood she was there because she *had* to be and not because she wanted to be. 'Also…' flushing, she bent to retrieve the large white box from the doorstep, which she held towards him '…Janette wanted you to have this.'

'What is it?' he questioned, eying the box warily.

A few random snowflakes fluttered onto her cheeks and she shuffled from one foot to the other, feeling acutely embarrassed by the cold lack of welcome in his eyes. Suddenly she understood the expression about wishing the ground would open up and swallow you. 'It's a cake.'

'A cake?' he echoed.

'We wanted to…well, it was Janette's idea, actually. She wanted to celebrate the sale of Kastelloes and so she asked me to bake you a cake.'

'And does she ask you to do this for all your purchasers?' he questioned silkily as he took the box from her. 'Or should I be flattered?'

Something about the sarcastic way he said it made Hollie's temper suddenly erupt. She had tried doing this in a polite and professional manner yet he still seemed so full of himself. So full of arrogant provocation and mockery. Did he think she'd concocted some kind of flimsy excuse just in order to see him? She wasn't *that* desperate. 'Christmas is supposed to be a time for giving, isn't it?' she retorted. 'Perhaps that was one of the reasons she asked me to do it. And you don't have to eat it, you know,' she added. 'You can always feed it to the birds. I'm sure they'd appreciate something to line their stomachs in this cold weather.'

'I'm sure they would,' he said. As if on cue, a flurry of snow came cascading down from the straining sky, straight onto her sleek head, and Maximo reluctantly acknowledged the growing tension inside him.

He had come to this ancient castle specifically to escape Christmas, because it was a festival he avoided wherever possible. It provided the ideal bolt-hole and he'd planned to spend a few days there before he had the building razed to the ground. He hadn't imagined that anybody would come near him and he hadn't wanted them to. Yet now Hollie Walker had turned up, reminding him of his harsh new reality. Forcing him to acknowledge the child growing in her belly—a fact which was complicated by the realisation that he would like nothing better than to take her into his arms and kiss her again. To strip her of her drab clothing and reveal the luscious body which lay beneath. To lose himself in her sweetness as he had done on that rain-lashed night.

His mouth twisted, because what would be the point of that? He was not going to be a part of her life, or her child's. He had given her the details of his lawyer, so she could be in no doubt that he would be more than generous. Because providing financially for Hollie and her baby was something he could do. The *only* thing he could do. A child needed love and he did not know how to give love. His heart was damaged—his emotions shredded. He had accepted that a long time ago.

So why not just sign the damned papers, enthuse over the damned cake and then send her on her way, no matter how much he hungered to recreate that night he'd spent in her arms? If he was cold and indifferent towards her, she would soon realise how much better off she was without a man like him. 'You'd better come inside,' he said.

'Don't worry. I'll be sure not to keep you for any longer than I have to.'

'Let's go to the library,' he said, shutting the door on the icy blast outside. 'Unlike most of the castle, at least it's warm in there.'

'Whatever,' she said, with a shrug.

Hollie's heart was heavy as she followed Maximo through the wood-panelled corridors, thinking he couldn't have been more unwelcoming if he'd tried. She thought how abrupt he seemed and she wished she weren't here. In fact, she wished she were anywhere but here—but the instant she entered the library, her concerns were briefly forgotten.

She'd only ever seen the place deserted, when Janette had brought her round to view it just before it went on the market. The fire exit signs from its days as a hotel were faded and the place had always appeared so lacklustre and uninspiring. But not today. Today she found herself noticing the perfect proportions of the room—the intricate carvings of cherubs and sailing ships, and the huge mullioned windows which overlooked the grounds. Was that Maximo's influence? she found herself wondering. Did he have the ability to transmute dull surroundings and turn them into a place which breathed beauty, as he had done the night when she'd taken him home?

Maybe it was just the roaring fire in the grate which had brought the ancient room to vibrant life—illuminating the detailing on the stone fireplace and the bare wall above it, which was just crying out for a painting. A rich landscape in oil, Hollie thought longingly. Or a portrait. You could put a comfortable chair underneath—two chairs, maybe—and sit there in the evenings watching the shadows fall. She felt a wistful wrench of her heart. Couldn't someone turn this castle into a home?

It was unlikely to be Maximo.

She turned to find him studying her, his black gaze fixed on her intently, as if he had never really seen her before. Hollie's heart missed a beat, because wasn't she feeling a bit like that herself? As if this were the first time they'd ever been alone. She felt *awkward* in his presence, which was slightly ridiculous, when you considered all the things they'd done together.

Or maybe it wasn't ridiculous at all. What did she know? She'd thought that what they'd shared had been intimacy, but she had been wrong. In her innocence she had confused sex with real closeness. But you could be naked in a man's arms and it counted for nothing, because right now Maximo Diaz seemed like a stranger. A stranger whose child she carried.

'What exactly do you want me to sign?' he questioned, putting the unopened box down on the table.

'It's right here.' Her hands were trembling as she scrabbled around inside her briefcase and she wondered if he'd noticed as she walked across the room towards him. 'It's the release form concerning the fixtures and fittings. It's just a formality.'

He was reading it. Of course he was. He wasn't the kind of man who would put his signature to something he hadn't studied first. And because he was reading it, it was taking much longer than she had anticipated.

The silence in the room seemed immense and Hollie pulled out her phone and began to look at it, as if there were loads of missed calls she needed to attend to, though in truth the screen was just a blur of mangled words. As a distraction technique it was pretty useless because she couldn't escape the troubled whirl of her thoughts as the minutes ticked slowly by. His dark head was bent and when eventually she heard the scratch of his pen, he looked up, his smile brief and perfunctory.

'I think that's everything you need.'

He can't wait to get rid of you.

He was rising from the chair and Hollie couldn't hold back her shiver as he handed her the document.

'If there's nothing more, I'll see you out.'

'There's really no need. I know my way around.'

'I insist.' He shot her a brief look and something

like pain filtered through his black eyes. 'How are you feeling?'

It might have been funny if it hadn't been so sad and Hollie only just managed to keep a burst of hysterical laughter from her lips. To say there was an elephant in the room didn't come close to it. Was that to be his only reference to the fact that she was pregnant? Because if so she was just going to have to deal with it. From somewhere she managed to produce a smile. 'I'm fine, thanks,' she said. 'The doctor seems very pleased with my progress so far.'

There was a pause. 'Look, I'm aware that my reaction to your news wasn't great and I apologise for that.'

His words were grudging rather than heartfelt, but Hollie told herself she must be generous in her response. 'No, it was hardly the stuff of dreams,' she said drily. 'But that's okay. It must have come as a terrible shock and at least you were being honest. And I'm over it now.'

'My lawyers tell me you haven't made contact yet.'

'No. I thought I'd wait until after Christmas now.'

He inclined his head. 'As you wish.'

As you wish?

Hollie had a whole catalogue of wishes, most of which were never going to come true. She wished he had a heart instead of a lump of cold steel lodged somewhere deep in his chest. She wished…

No. Only a fool would ever wish for love from such an unsuitable candidate.

They had reached the hall and he was opening the door and all Hollie wanted was to get away from him and the way he was making her feel, when his terse exclamation startled her.

'Es imposible!'

Hollie followed his gaze and looked outside. Her Spanish was limited to about three words which involved asking for a beer, but even she understood that what he'd just said wasn't true, because it wasn't impossible at all. She felt the jump of her heart. She'd been so busy with her thoughts that she'd barely noticed the time passing, or the increased snowfall. But from here she was aware of how quickly the weather had closed in, and now they seemed to be in a complete white-out.

The landscape had been utterly transformed. Trees, grass and bushes were coated with a mantle of white, which sparkled like diamonds in the fading violet light. The thick fall had turned the place into a winter fairy tale—but one with an underlying threat because, outwardly, everything had changed. No footsteps up the lane. It was as if she'd never been there.

Hollie had only ever thought of snow as a positive thing—as pretty, white and fluffy—but now she saw it as an obstacle, barring her way out of there. And there was no sign of it stopping. She stared up into the darkening sky and uttered a soft curse beneath her breath. All she wanted was to get back to her little cottage because, although it might not amount to very much, at least it was *home*.

'Where's your taxi?' he demanded.

She shrugged. 'I got a lift here and I was planning to walk back.'

He made a soft curse beneath his breath. 'I would take you myself except that I've dismissed the chauffeur for the holidays and he's taken the car.'

'It's fine,' she said, between gritted teeth, thinking that she'd rather walk home barefoot than be driven home by *him*. 'I've been cooped up in the office all morning, and a bit of snow won't kill me.' With a grimace of stark realisation, Hollie stared down at her feet. 'These boots weren't exactly made for walking, but I guess they'll have to do.'

'Are you out of your mind?' he snapped. 'You can't possibly walk home in this.'

'Watch me.'

'I don't think so. You're pregnant, remember?'

'I'm hardly likely to forget, am I?'

'Do you make a habit of being rescued from bad weather, Hollie?' he demanded. 'Don't you think it's time you invested in one of those clever phone apps?'

'Oh, go to hell!' she snapped back, taking a defiant step forward and immediately sinking into a deep white drift which came almost to the top of her boots. And suddenly Maximo's hands were on her waist and he was lifting her clean out of the snow, and she was staring up into the hard glitter of his black eyes. And wasn't it crazy that, in the midst of all her complicated emotions, her overriding feeling was the hungry throb of her blood in response to his touch? 'Go to hell,' she repeated weakly.

His velvety voice filtered over her skin. 'Even hell would reject a man like me.'

'Please put me down,' she said. 'I want to go home.'

'Well, you can't. You're not going anywhere right now. Not when it's like this. You're going to have to stay here for the time being.' He lowered her to her feet. 'Unless that's what you had in mind all along?'

She moved even further away from him, though that did little to ease the furious punch of her heart. 'Are you serious? Are you arrogant enough to think I'd deliberately get myself stranded here like this?'

He shrugged. 'Only you know the answer to that, Hollie. But if you're asking whether I think a woman is capable of such manipulation, then I'm afraid the answer has to be yes.'

'Why, you…*cynic*,' she breathed.

'You think so? I prefer to call it realism. But that's irrelevant.' He moved towards the door, his muscular body all honed and rippling strength. 'And rather than standing here debating my perceived defects of character, you'd better come inside, out of the cold.'

CHAPTER SIX

MAXIMO SHUT THE door with more force than he intended, his heart racing with…what? Anger at being stuck with an uninvited guest at the worst time of the year? Yes, there was that. But Hollie was not just any uninvited guest. He stared down at the mutinous tremble of her lips and felt the shimmer of something indefinable spearing at his heart. She was the mother of his child, he reminded himself grimly. A child he had never wanted. Because why would he wish to pass on his cold and emotionless genes to an innocent baby?

Yet his feelings of claustrophobia were complicated by a sensation which threatened to derail his intention to keep his distance from the woman he had seduced, and no matter how firmly he spoke to himself, it was having precisely no effect on him. Because every time he looked at Hollie Walker, he felt that same powerful kick of desire. In spite of everything, he still wanted her. He wanted her badly and yet he still couldn't work out why. He liked his women hard-edged. Tough and sexy. Women who knew the score—not wide-eyed innocents, with lips which trembled when you kissed them.

He preferred considered sex—a careful coupling rather than wild passion which ran the risk of taking a man hostage. He drew his boundaries from the outset. He preferred to be in the driving seat when it came to relationships and women were so eager for his body and his company that they invariably acceded to his demands. Yet with Hollie Walker, hadn't he already broken one of his self-imposed rules? They said a woman was a mystery until you bedded her and once that happened, she inevitably lost some of that allure. That had always been the case before, so why wasn't it happening now?

Why did he want to discover more about her? And why the hell was he experiencing an overwhelming need to tumble her down and cover her soft body with the hot, hard heat of his own until she cried out his name? She might currently be glaring at him as if he were the devil incarnate, but her anger didn't quite mask her own desire. No. Not at all. The faint flush of her cheeks and the darkening of her spectacular grey eyes was a pretty reliable indicator that she was far from immune to *him*. And since they were stuck with each other until the snow melted, perhaps it might be a good idea to capitalise on that potent sexual chemistry.

They had to do *something* to occupy themselves during the long hours ahead and tomorrow was Christmas Day—a holiday which up until now had always been something he just needed to survive, but now he could see the possibility of transforming it into something else.

Something erotic.

The clench in his gut was sweetly pervasive until the split second when he noticed the flash of vulnerability which had crossed her pale face and silently he remonstrated with himself, forcing himself to listen to reason.

You don't have to have sex with her. You just have to provide shelter until the weather breaks and get through the next few hours.

'I'll show you where you can sleep,' he said tightly.

'I'm sure that won't be necessary,' she said, equally tightly. 'I'm not planning on staying any longer than I need to.'

'You'll stay until it's safe to return and that certainly won't be before nightfall.'

Their eyes met in a silent clash of wills, until eventually she backed down and nodded.

'Then it seems I have no choice.'

'That's right,' he agreed softly. 'You don't. Now come with me.'

Hollie felt chewed up as she trailed behind Maximo up the curving stone staircase which led to the upstairs floor of the chilly castle. She was scared. Scared of the way he made her feel. Scared of wanting to touch him instead of needing to push him away. Because he didn't want her. *He didn't want her.* And that was something she shouldn't forget. His dismay on discovering she was trapped here might have been almost comical to observe, if it hadn't been so hurtful. But she guessed that nobody could ever accuse Maximo Diaz of being duplicitous. He was honest to a fault, which had to be a good thing. And since she was here—maybe she just needed to make the best of it. To look on the bright side. She pressed her lips together.

For both their sakes.

He was pushing open the door of one of the bedrooms and as Hollie stepped inside she was aware of a further drop in temperature. The bed was bare and the room largely empty—there was nothing in the way of decorative furnishing to make it seem inviting or attractive. It certainly wasn't going to be a fairy-tale Christmas Eve, not by any stretch of the imagination.

'You'll find linen in the big wooden cupboard just along the corridor,' he advised, his dark brows knitting together, as if he had just noticed her shiver. 'You're cold?'

'A bit.'

'Let me see what I can do. I've never seen anything quite so archaic as what passes for a heating system here.'

'Don't you have any staff with you?' she questioned curiously.

Black eyebrows were elevated in mocking query. 'You think I travel around with a retinue of servants?'

She shrugged. 'You're a rich man. Apparently, that's what rich men do. And you *do* have a chauffeur.'

'*Si.* I do. But the answer is no, I am completely on my own. Because surely a man is not a true man if he cannot fend for himself. If he cannot live independently of his staff.'

'Christmas is not a time for independence,' she said firmly. 'It's a time for family.'

'And will your family be missing you, Hollie?' he questioned suddenly. 'Is that why you are so eager to get back?'

'I have no family,' she said, deciding it wouldn't be diplomatic or wise to tell him that her desire to get away had been all about his effect on her. Baldly, she gave him the bare facts, the way she always did, just so they could get the inevitable mechanical sympathy out of the way. 'Both my parents are dead.'

'Snap,' he said softly.

It wasn't what she'd been expecting and Hollie almost wished he hadn't told her that, because that was the stupid thing about the mind—it took you down false paths, based on very flimsy evidence. If she wasn't careful it would be easy to start imagining they had something in common, because they were both orphans. When she knew and he knew that they had absolutely nothing in common, other than an inconvenient sexual chemistry and a baby neither of them had planned.

'At least nobody's going to miss us!' she observed brightly, wishing it didn't please her so much to see him smile in response. But the curve of his lips lasted only a second, as though this man was not comfortable with smiling.

'I'll leave you to get settled in,' he said abruptly. 'I'll be downstairs. Come and find me when you've finished. Take as long as you like.'

Settling in seemed a rather over-ambitious term for getting used to such spartan accommodation, but after Maximo had left, Hollie tried to make the bedroom as comfortable as possible. There were no sheets, but she hunted down several mismatched velvet throws and a thick eiderdown, which provided a colourful display against the quiet grey hues of the faded walls. And thankfully she was *used* to sleeping in a chilly bedroom.

The nearby bathroom was ancient, with a noisy cistern and a vast, old-fashioned bath—but the water was piping hot. She washed her hands with a bar of rock-hard soap then stared into the rather mottled mirror above the sink. She was expecting her appearance to come as a shock, but to her surprise her eyes were shining and her cheeks were pink and glowing. She brushed her hair, tempted to leave it loose because wouldn't that provide some essential warmth around her neck and shoulders? But something stopped her and it was the memory of Maximo using a single strand of it as a rope, just before he'd kissed her. Because those kinds of memories weren't helpful. Not helpful at all. Carefully, she wound it into a tight chignon and pinned it into place, before heading downstairs to find Maximo.

He wasn't in the library, but she could smell the aroma of food cooking and Hollie made her way through a series of maze-like corridors towards the kitchen. She could hear movement but when she walked in, the sight which greeted her was the last thing she had expected. What *had* she expected? She wasn't sure—but it certainly wasn't to see the Spanish tycoon with his back to her, his black sweater rolled up to his elbows as he stirred something.

Did she make a sound? Was that why he turned around, his olive skin gleaming from the heat of the hob? And Hollie could do nothing about the instant wrench of her heart, as if she were registering his gorgeousness for the very first time. Because Maximo, holding up a wooden spoon as the conductor of an orchestra might hold a baton, looked insanely sexy. Maybe her hormones were making her respond to him this way. Because right then he looked like the carer and provider. The alpha man. The hunter. The father of her baby. Beneath her sweater she felt her breasts tighten and wondered if he'd noticed. Would that account for the almost imperceptible narrowing of his eyes and the sudden tension which stilled his magnificent body so that he looked almost poised to strike?

'Gosh,' she said.

'Gosh?' he echoed, his sardonic tone easing a little of the tension in the air. 'Am I to take that as a very English word of surprise?'

'I suppose I am a bit surprised,' she admitted. 'I didn't have you down as a budding chef.'

'Less of the budding, more of the accomplished.'

'Of course. Silly of me to forget that you probably excel in everything you turn your hand to.'

'You're getting the hang of me, Hollie.'

'Who taught you to cook?'

'I'm self-taught.'

'Wow.' She blew a silent whistle. 'Now I'm even more impressed.'

'Why wouldn't I teach myself how to cook?' he questioned. 'As I told you, my independence is important to me.' His black eyes glittered a challenge at her. 'And isn't your assumption that I'm breaking some sort of mould rather sexist?'

Was it? Hollie wasn't sure. As he turned back

to the hob, the only thing she was certain of was a stupid sense of yearning as she feasted her eyes on the black tendrils of hair which brushed against his neck. She didn't want to feel wistful but it was difficult not to. Because if they'd been a real couple they might have done stuff like this—cooked meals and flirted a little. They might have gone out on a few dates, instead of letting passion lead them to a one-night stand with massive consequences. But she wasn't the type of woman Maximo dated, she reminded herself fiercely. She'd seen photos of his girlfriends on the Internet and she was nothing like any of them. She just happened to be a warm and willing body who had made herself available on a night when he'd obviously wanted company.

But those were pointless thoughts. Negative thoughts she wasn't going to entertain. Instead Hollie watched as Maximo chopped onions with rather terrifying dexterity and realised he hadn't been exaggerating about his prowess in the kitchen. 'So what are you cooking?' she asked.

'It's a variation of a dish called *cocido montañéas*. Mountain stew. It comes from northern Spain. From Cantabria.'

'And is that where you come from?'

'It is.' He sliced a wooden spoon through the thick mixture, clearly more comfortable discussing the meal than details about his birthplace. 'It's more of a winter soup really, with pork and chorizo and beans and greens and wine and garlic and pretty much anything else you can find to throw in.'

'It's not…'

'Not?' He turned round again as her words tailed off, only this time his gleaming black gaze pierced through her like a sword. 'Not what, Hollie?'

'Well, it's not the kind of food I can imagine someone like you eating, let alone cooking.'

'Why not?'

Hollie traced her finger along a deep gouge in the ancient table and wondered how long ago it had been put there and by whom. 'It's more I imagine the food a labourer might eat.'

'And I'm no labourer?'

She smiled at the preposterousness of this. 'Obviously not.'

'Maybe,' he said softly. 'But once I was.'

She glanced up from the table, watching as he put a lid on the pot and turned the heat down low. 'You? A labourer?'

Maximo didn't answer immediately, amazed he'd given her an opening to pursue this particular topic because discussions about his past were something he vetoed. Especially with lovers. Women *always* asked questions and he understood why. Knowledge was power and the more you knew about someone, the closer you could presume your relationship to be. Except that any 'closeness' his lovers presumed was all inside their heads. Usually he recommended they consult the Internet if they wanted to discover more about him, confident they'd find out only what he wanted them to know—having successfully kept his online profile deliberately sparse, by employing an IT expert who made sure that happened.

His past was private and his alone—and the only time he connected with it was during this ritual he followed most Christmases, when he cooked up the kind of food which would never feature on the menu of any of the fancy restaurants he frequented these days. At Christmas he went back to basics. He did it because it reminded him of who he had been and where he had come from, and usually it was enough to make him satisfied with his lot and to remind him what he *didn't* want from life.

But something had happened which had changed the way he thought about everything, and though it pained him to admit it—it all stemmed from his mother's recent passing. Didn't seem to matter that he didn't *want* to be affected by the death of a woman he had despised. Fact was, he was. Ever since it had happened he'd felt…disconnected. Like a tethered balloon whose string had just been cut, leaving him drifting aimlessly and without direction. As if all the money and power he had acquired along the way suddenly meant nothing. Was that why he had taken this provincial office worker to bed and lost himself in a storm of passion so all-pervasive that it had left him feeling dazed and confused the next morning? As if, for the first time in his life, it had felt as if he'd come home.

Wasn't that why he hadn't contacted her again? Because he didn't like the way she made him feel, or because he didn't trust those feelings?

He didn't know and he didn't care and that was why he had walked away. Why he had resisted the surprising desire to contact her again. And time was great for taking the urgency out of desire. It had been easy to lose himself in work and travel and to allow the many projects he juggled to take over his life. To forget about that night and the woman who had temporarily made him lose control.

Yet now, as he stared into the wide grey eyes which were fixed on his, he found himself wanting to tell her stuff. Nothing too deep. No, definitely not that. But it would amuse him to reveal his beginnings to her, to show her some of the real man beneath the fancy patina. Would take his mind off the persistent urge to pull her into his arms and start kissing her, which would complicate his life in a way it didn't need complicating.

'Yes, I was a labourer,' he said. 'And if you know my roots you might be able to understand why. I was the only child of a single mother, and money was scarce. I remember being hungry—always hungry. My need to get food took precedence over schoolwork and the local school wasn't up to much anyway. And when I was fourteen, I started working on the roads.'

'Fourteen?' she breathed, her eyes growing even wider. 'Wow. Is that even *legal*?'

'I doubt it.' He shrugged. 'But there weren't so many checks back then. It was a different kind of world. The guy who owned the construction site didn't know how old I was and if they had, they probably wouldn't have cared.'

'You mean you lied about your age?' she questioned, as if that were important to her.

'I let them believe what they wanted to believe. That's mostly what people do in life, Hollie— haven't you discovered that by now? I was big and strong for my age and looked much older than I was, and it was easy to let my work speak for itself. I started out with a pick and shovel. Breaking up rocks with a big hammer and trying not to inhale the dust. I learnt a lot about construction.' He gave a short laugh. 'But I learnt plenty more about human nature.'

'In what way?'

Her voice was soft. Way too soft to resist—and for some reason, Maximo didn't even try.

'I learnt how to fight,' he admitted. 'I learnt how a man can lose everything through drink, and that gambling is nothing but a short journey to ruin. But mostly I learnt that I didn't want to hang round doing that kind of work for ever.'

'No, I can imagine you didn't. So how did you make the leap, from being a—?'

'Labourer?' Her head was bent as she traced all the scratches on the table with the tip of her finger, as if she were trying not to meet his gaze. And wasn't there a bit of him which was glad about that? Because those beautiful grey eyes were cool and searching and it wasn't easy to ignore their candid gaze.

'It wasn't rocket science,' he continued. 'I made sure I was always the first to arrive and the last to leave and I saved every euro I could to buy my first digger. Eventually that one digger became five, and then twenty—and soon I was the sub-contractor of choice for the big boys.' He gave a short laugh. 'Until I became one of the big boys myself. I started building roads and then railways, and I never really looked back.' Most emphatically he had not looked back.

She absorbed all this in silence for a moment. 'It's not—'

'Not what you expected?' he supplied acidly. 'You imagined I was born with the Spanish equivalent of a silver spoon in my mouth? *Nacer en cuna de oro*. That I grew up with money?'

'Something like that. You seem very comfortable with your wealth. Comfortable in your own skin.'

'Thank you,' he said gravely, and was aware of the warm approbation in his voice as he said it. Her look of surprise indicated she'd heard it too, but then she was unaware that she had just paid him a great compliment—perhaps the greatest compliment of all. For hadn't that been what he had strived for above all else? *To feel comfortable in his own skin.*

But then she ruined it.

'And you have a kind of—I don't know.' She wriggled her shoulders. 'A kind of *aristocratic* look about you.'

Maximo's lips clamped shut, telling himself to be grateful that her perceptive observation had brought him to his senses at last. What was the *matter* with him? Hadn't he been just about to tell her the rest of his pitiful story, lulled by her soft voice and seeking eyes? And why—just because his estranged mother was dead and his equilibrium had temporarily been disturbed?

Hadn't he spent the last two decades eradicating those memories—only to almost blurt them out to a woman who already had too much power over him? Because her pregnancy gave Hollie Walker undue influence in his life, he recognised suddenly—and she could use that influence any way she saw fit.

He gave the pot another stir. He had carefully controlled his image for most of his life. He never gave interviews, never let people too close. He worked hard and played hard and donated generously to charity—and for these qualities he was mostly admired and envied in equal measure. But of himself he gave nothing away. Even during his longest relationships—and none of those had ever been what you'd call lengthy—he had never been anything less than guarded. Hadn't that been part of his appeal—that women saw him as an enigma and a challenge and themselves as the one who would break down those high barriers with which he had surrounded himself?

But Hollie was different. She couldn't help but be different. She was carrying his baby and, inevitably, that was going to cause ripples of curiosity in the circles in which he moved. Sooner or later people were going to find out that this unknown English-woman was pregnant with his child. She would be able to present herself to the world however she saw fit. As a victim, if she so desired. And he would have absolutely no control over that.

He felt the sudden knot in his stomach. He had already told her plenty about himself, but of her he knew nothing. Nothing at all. Wasn't it time he did? Not because he particularly cared what made her tick, but because he needed to redress that balance of knowledge.

He pulled out the stool opposite hers and sat down. 'What about you?' he questioned, carelessly.

'Me?'

'I've told you how I started out. Now it's your turn.'

Hollie hesitated. He had divulged much more

than she'd expected, though she'd noticed that his story had stopped very abruptly. But he had still surprised her and maybe if he hadn't been so forthcoming she might have brushed over her own background, because it wasn't much to write home about, was it? Even so, it was more than a little distracting to have him sitting so close, making her acutely aware of all the latent power in his muscular body and the devilish gleam of his ebony eyes.

'I was the only child of a single mother, too,' she began and saw a muscle begin working at his temple, as if he thought she was grasping for things they had in common and was irritated by it. Instantly, she sought to emphasise the differences between them. 'We weren't exactly poor, but we weren't exactly rich either. My father...'

'What about your father?' he probed.

She shrugged. 'Well, to be honest, I never knew him very well. He was a bit of a womaniser, I guess. Good-looking. Easy company. One of those men who want to have their cake and eat it. He was a sales manager and so travelled around the area a lot. He had several different lovers, although only one child, as far as I know. He'd tell my mother he loved her and he'd move in with us for a bit and then...' She shrugged. 'I don't know if having a baby cramped his style, or whether he found it stultifying that the whole household always seemed to revolve around him. But the more my mother ran

"4 for 4" MINI-SURVEY

We are prepared to **REWARD** you with 4 FREE Books and Free Gifts for completing our MINI SURVEY!

Sizzling Romance

Passionate Romance

You'll get up to...

4 FREE BOOKS & FREE GIFTS

ust for participating in our Mini Survey!

Get Up To 4 Free Books!

Dear Reader,

IT'S A FACT: if you answer 4 quick questions, we'll send you 4 FREE REWARDS from each series you try!

Try **Harlequin® Desire** books featuring the worlds of the American elite with juicy plot twists, delicious sensuality and intriguing scandal.

Try **Harlequin Presents®** Larger-Print books featuring the glamourous lives of royals and billionaires in a world of exotic locations, where passion knows no bounds.

Or **TRY BOTH!**

I'm not kidding you. As a leading publisher of women's fiction, we value your opinions... and your time. That's why we are prepared to reward you handsomely for completing our mini-survey. In fact, we have 4 Free Rewards for you, including 2 free books and 2 free gifts from each series you try!

Thank you for participating in our survey,

Pam Powers

To get your 4 FREE REWARDS:
Complete the survey below and return the insert today to receive up to 4 FREE BOOKS and FREE GIFTS guaranteed!

"4 for 4" MINI-SURVEY

1 Is reading one of your favorite hobbies?

☐ YES ☐ NO

2 Do you prefer to read instead of watch TV?

☐ YES ☐ NO

3 Do you read newspapers and magazines?

☐ YES ☐ NO

4 Do you enjoy trying new book series with FREE BOOKS?

☐ YES ☐ NO

Please send me my Free Rewards, consisting of **2 Free Books from each series I select** and **Free Mystery Gifts**. I understand that I am under no obligation to buy anything, as explained on the back of this card.

❏ **Harlequin Desire®** (225/326 HDL GQ3X)
❏ **Harlequin Presents® Larger-Print** (176/376 HDL GQ3X)
❏ **Try Both** (225/326 & 176/376 HDL GQ4A)

FIRST NAME	LAST NAME

ADDRESS

APT.#	CITY

STATE/PROV.	ZIP/POSTAL CODE

EMAIL ❏ Please check this box if you would like to receive newsletters and promotional emails from Harlequin Enterprises ULC and its affiliates. You can unsubscribe anytime.

HD/HP-520-MS20

round after him, the more he seemed to despise her. So they'd have a big row and he'd move out and then the whole cycle would start again.'

'That must have been tough on you,' he observed slowly.

'Not really.' Hollie slipped into her best *every-cloud-has-a-silver-lining* attitude. 'It's true that Mum used to go to pieces every time, but it's how I taught myself how to cook, and…'

'Go on,' he said, the faintest of smiles touching the edges of his mouth.

She picked up the story again, thinking that nobody ever really asked her stuff like this. 'One day my father just stopped contacting her and we never found out what happened to him. Like you said, things were different in those days and there was no social media to be able to track someone down. My mum never really got over it and after she died, I sold her little house and went to catering college. Long story short, I made a friend there and used the rest of my savings to go into business with her—we opened a tea shop in London.'

'But? I sense there's a but coming.'

He was insightful, she thought—or maybe such a successful businessman was always going to have an instinct for a duff business venture. 'My partner borrowed a whole load of money on the business and couldn't pay it back.'

'That's theft,' he observed acidly.

'She *meant* to pay it back,' she defended. 'But that was never going to happen and I couldn't bear to waste any more time, or make any more bad memories by chasing her through the small courts. Anyway, we'd chosen a hopeless location. It was more a hip coffee shop sort of area and not really suited to a venue which was serving dinky plates of scones, with cream and jam. It's why I came to Devon, which *is* that kind of place. It's why, no matter what happens, I'm glad you came here too, Maximo.'

He looked startled. 'You are?'

'Yes, I am. Not because of the baby, because I know that's bad news for you.' She ignored the pained expression on his face but resolutely carried on. 'It wasn't meant to happen, but it did—and I will do everything to make sure our child has the best possible life I can give them. And I've lived with a man who didn't want to be a father, which is why I can cope with the fact you don't want to be involved. It's better that way. Better that we're upfront about things from the beginning so everyone knows where they stand—'

'Hollie—'

'No, please let me finish.' She drew a deep breath and stared straight into his fathoms-deep eyes, thinking how thick and black the lashes were. 'What makes me glad is the fact that you've bought Kastelloes, because you'll be injecting life back into

this town and local community. So my business—
and every other business in Trescombe—will benefit.' He got up quickly to attend to his cooking, an
uncomfortable expression crossing his face, and she
wondered if she was boring him. 'Gosh, it's seven
o'clock already,' she observed, sneaking a glance
at her watch. 'Only five more hours to go and it'll
be Christmas Day!'

'I can hardly wait,' he said sarcastically.

She watched as he finished cooking the meal,
wishing she could tear her eyes away from the
graceful agility of his movements and the way his
black jeans clung to the hard thrust of his buttocks.
But she couldn't. And all the while she was becoming aware of the four walls which surrounded
them and the fact that they were completely alone
in this beautiful, desolate building. She could feel
tension between them mounting—like dark layers
of something tantalising, building and building into
the promise of something unbearably sweet.

'Let's eat,' he said suddenly.

But his face was still tense as he began to serve
up the soup, his shadow seeming to swamp her in an
all-consuming darkness. And somehow his abrupt
words managed to destroy the fragile harmony
which had briefly existed between them.

CHAPTER SEVEN

HOLLIE SHIVERED AS she lay huddled beneath the heap of the velvet throws, wiggling her toes to stop them from freezing. It was so *quiet*. Nothing to listen to except the sound of the distant church bells in nearby Trescombe. Nothing to distract her from the thought that Maximo was sleeping just along the corridor and that felt weird. Was he thinking about her and her predicament, or was he fast asleep and oblivious to the presence of his unwanted guest? She cocked her ear as the twelfth and final bell faded into the silent night, announcing to the world that Christmas day had finally arrived.

Some Christmas! She was stuck in a cold, almost empty castle with a man who didn't want her there. She turned her pillow over and bashed it with her fist. Didn't matter how many sheep she tried to count, she just couldn't sleep. In fact, she had dozed only fitfully since she'd retired to bed just after ten last night, leaving Maximo downstairs, working in the library.

Their shared supper had been *awkward*, to say the least. Oh, the food had been delicious—no doubt about that. Maximo's Cantabrian mountain stew had hit the spot and the tycoon had waited on her in a way she suspected was totally out of character. She had been impressed by his culinary skills and had said so. But Hollie hadn't been impervious to the unspoken words which had seemed to dangle in the air like invisible baubles. Just as she'd been unable to ignore the spiralling tension which curled like smoke in the base of her stomach whenever he came near.

But last night had been about more than sexual chemistry and, although his powerful presence had been impossible to ignore, Hollie had learnt a little more about the father of her child. It had been an illuminating insight to discover that his wealth hadn't been handed to him on a plate, but he was a self-made man, and that revelation had made her feel an undoubted respect towards him. Yet afterwards it was as if he regretted having told her anything at all, because when she had tried to ask him about growing up in those harsh circumstances, he had very firmly changed the subject. And after that, things had become a little stilted.

It hadn't exactly helped that she had nothing to sleep in and when she'd plucked up courage to ask

Maximo if he had a pyjama top she could borrow, he had stared at her as if she had taken leave of her senses.

'Are you crazy?' he'd questioned, black eyes narrowed. 'I never wear anything in bed.'

It had proved yet one more awkward moment in a whole series of them and in Hollie's opinion, that was far too much information to take on board, in the circumstances. Berating her naïve stupidity and hiding her sudden blush by leaping to her feet, she had escaped upstairs and run herself a bath—more to get warm than anything else. But when she had returned to her room she had found a T-shirt lying on top of the velvet heap of bedcovers, which Maximo must have left there for her. A black T-shirt with the word *Legend* inscribed across the front. Pulling it on, she had momentarily revelled in the feel of the soft material against her clean skin—even though the garment had swamped her. And wasn't she aware—on some fundamental level—that she got a kick out of wearing it because *he* had worn it, too?

She tossed and turned as the minutes continued to tick slowly by. She looked at her watch to note that midnight had become one o'clock and she was as restless as before and so, wrapping one of the velvet throws around herself, she went to the window and gazed outside. And despite everything, she couldn't hold back the sigh of wonder which escaped from her lips because outside was the most perfect scene she could imagine—like an illustration from a book about winter.

The snow had stopped falling and the moon was huge in the sky, bathing the milky landscape in a bright and silvery light. Against the frosty stillness of the landscape, the tall shapes of the trees rose ghostly and beautiful and for a moment Holly just drank it all in until the dryness in her throat reminded her that she was thirsty. Why hadn't she thought to bring a drink to bed with her?

She stood very still and listened but could hear nothing and surely Maximo must be fast asleep by now. Carefully opening the door to avoid making any noise, she crept along the corridor, clutching her makeshift cloak around her. The whisper of velvet brushing against the stone steps was the only sound she could hear and quietly she made her way to the kitchen, turning the switch on so that it flooded with light. It was neat and clean, all the debris from dinner tidied away. Maximo had obviously cleared up after she went to bed. He really *was* independent she thought, scrolling back through those rare memories of her father to realise that not once had he ever lifted a finger to help her mother.

She poured herself a glass of water and thirstily gulped it down before pouring another and switching off the light. And although the castle was dark and very quiet, Hollie wasn't in the least bit spooked—because the walls felt friendly. She wondered if other women, like her, had wandered these stone corridors in the dead of night and wondered how they were going to cope with an unknown future.

Lost in thought, she had almost reached the end of the passageway when a figure suddenly emerged from the shadows and Hollie jumped. Water arced and splashed against the stone wall and as the glass slipped from her fingers Maximo lunged forward to catch it—cradling the intact vessel in the palm of his hand like a professional cricketer who had just made a sensational catch.

'You scared the life out of me!' she accused, aware that his hair was ruffled as if he'd hurriedly dragged his sweater over his head and that the top button of his jeans was undone.

'I didn't mean to alarm you. I couldn't sleep and I heard something moving downstairs, or rather someone, so I threw on some clothes and came down to investigate.' His shuttered gaze flicked over her. 'You'd better get back upstairs,' he added, and suddenly his voice was tinged with harshness. 'It's cold.'

Hollie nodded but she didn't move. She *couldn't* move. It was as if she had suddenly forgotten how to use her legs.

'It's cold everywhere,' she whispered. 'I've been awake for hours.'

His eyes narrowed and a look of intense calculation darkened his already shadowed features. He looked as if he were fighting some silent inner battle and when he nodded his head, Hollie couldn't decide whether he had won, or lost.

'Maybe we should try and do something about that,' he said. 'What do you think?'

His soft question slid over her skin, snaring her with threads of silk. And he was studying her with that absorbed and shadowed gaze, which was making her grow weak. And all the time, raw desire was pulsing around them, like a living being. Hollie felt breathless. Poised on the edge of something—but she didn't know the rules of this game. She didn't know how to play. 'That depends what you had in mind,' she stumbled.

He smiled. A slow and speculative smile. A smile no sane woman could have resisted. 'There are any number of options. We could go upstairs and I could lend you another T-shirt. We could see if we can find any more of those velvet wraps you seem so fond of. Or you could share my bed and get warm that way. It's up to you. It's your call, Hollie.'

Maybe if he'd asked that same question during daylight hours when he'd made it plain she was an unwelcome guest, then Hollie might have refused. But the darkness had added a strange layer of anonymity, as well as enhancing her already aroused senses. And it was Christmas morning, wasn't it?

A time of magic and secret wishes, when anything could happen. She sensed he wouldn't judge her if she said yes, because this was a time out of life and she wanted it. She wanted it very badly.

'Yes, please,' she said simply.

'Which?'

'You know which.'

He made a low growling noise beneath his breath, as if her easy capitulation had pleased him. Then he put the empty glass down on the stone floor, very carefully, and took her in his arms. He brushed her hair from her cheeks, looking down at her for a moment, his gaze crystalline and hard. She'd thought he might kiss her, but he didn't. Instead, he laced his fingers through hers and led her towards the stairs. It felt very grown-up but…it also felt very disappointing and it wasn't until they had reached the upstairs floor that Hollie raised her face to his in question. Because hadn't she secretly been longing for the ultimate castle fantasy of Maximo sweeping her up into his arms and carrying her to his lair?

'You want to know why I didn't carry you this time?' he guessed.

'Yes.' Hollie nodded, marvelling at his perception even as she resented it. Just how many women had he carried to his bed over the years? she wondered.

'Because you're pregnant,' he admitted. 'And I'm terrified of dropping you.'

It was a surprisingly tender admission and Hollie felt her skin grow warm. 'You're way too strong to drop me—and I'm not made of glass, Maximo.'

'I wouldn't bring up the subject of glass right now if I were you.'

His teasing broke a little of the tension until he stared down at her again, his expression dark and unfathomable, and she could see a pulse beating wildly at his temple. 'But since we're on the flat again...'

And this time he *did* pick her up, striding along the corridor to a room just beyond her own, kicking open the door and giving rampant life to her foolish fantasies. It was a room a little larger than her own and just as sparsely furnished, though the bed was much bigger. But Hollie barely noticed the equally haphazard bedclothes, or the thick paperback which was lying open on the locker. All she could see was the man who was lowering her onto the mattress, his aristocratic features dark and shuttered as he made sure she was covered by a feather-soft eiderdown, before stripping his clothes off.

She lay and watched as he peeled off his shirt, his skin gleaming like living metal in the bright moonlight which streamed in through the windows. She observed the line of black hair which arrowed down from his chest to his navel and as he began to slide the zip down, he lifted his head to slant her the sexiest smile she'd ever seen.

'Does it turn you on to watch me undress?' he murmured.

Hollie nodded. She liked that he wasn't treating her as a novice, which essentially she was. Last time they'd had sex it had all been so new and so incredible—as if she hadn't been able to believe that someone like Maximo was in bed with someone like her. But while she might be new to all this, even she could acknowledge the undeniable chemistry which burned between them and she was determined to enjoy every second of what came next. She wasn't going to long for the impossible or wish things had been different. That ship had sailed. She was going to live in the now.

The mattress dipped as he came to lie beside her, taking the baggy hem of the T-shirt she was still wearing and running the tip of his finger over it. 'You have me at something of a disadvantage,' he murmured. 'You're still wearing this, while I am completely naked.'

'Surely it's me that's at a disadvantage,' she returned, lifting her arms above her head without being asked so that he could peel off the offending garment and drop it to one side of the bed.

Maximo pulled her into his arms, brushing aside the thick fall of her silky hair as he pressed his lips into her neck. He hadn't thought this would happen. God knew, he hadn't intended for it to happen—but in the end she had proved too much of a temptation and, besides, which of them was he protecting by resisting something they obviously both wanted? Not her, who was so hungry for him that she was writhing against him like a siren, her breath warm and fast against his skin. Nor himself, either. After all, the damage had already been done and she was pregnant. And if that was a cynical way of looking at it, so what?

He began to explore her body, reacquainting himself with her soft curves and delicious flesh, his fingers sliding over her silky skin. He cupped her breasts in his palms, thinking how full they were—much fuller than last time.

Was that because of the baby?

A rush of something he didn't recognise roared through his blood but deliberately, he blocked it.

He wasn't going to think about the baby. The only thing he was going to think about was pleasure.

So he concentrated on employing every sensual skill he had learnt, tempering blatant provocation with the tantalising whisper of soft promise. So that while his rock-hard erection was pushing against her belly, he was kissing her eyelids, her cheeks, her neck and her ears, making her wait until finally he allowed his lips to plunder hers. Was it the little cry of bliss she gave which made him feel as if he were drowning? As if she were drawing him into some unknown place of dark, sweet honey.

'You are…*deliciosa.*'

'Delicious?' she guessed.

'You are fluent in Spanish now, are you, Hollie?' But as she opened her mouth to doubtless make some equally flippant reply, he kissed away the answer, reaching down to slide his finger between her silken folds, enjoying her gasped frustration as he brought her to the edge of orgasm, over and over again. Only when he could bear his own exquisite torture no longer did he position himself to enter her at last—though more slowly and carefully than he had ever done before. And didn't that make him feel…?

What?

He didn't know and he didn't care because his thoughts were being scatter-gunned by Hollie clenching hard around him, her back arching like a bow as she spasmed, and then he too was jerking helplessly in her arms.

For a while there was no sound other than their ragged sighs, and then she drifted her lips to his cheek.

'Maximo,' she murmured huskily.

'Don't move,' he instructed unsteadily, because already he was growing hard inside her again. 'Stay exactly where you are.'

'I have no intention of going anywhere.'

He gave a soft laugh as he began to move and, while the second time was just as amazing, the third almost defied definition, leaving him gloriously sated and replete.

'I've never done it without protection before,' he observed after a while, lying back against the rumpled bedclothes, his skin warm with satisfaction.

'So that's a first?'

'Well, by my reckoning, it's actually the second.'

His head tipped back against the pillow as she giggled and he must have slept, because when next he opened his eyes, the bright light of a winter's morning had replaced the silvery moonlight of the previous night. He lay there for a moment in silence, aware of Hollie's head on his shoulder—her hair spread out over his chest like satin. He stared down at the twin crescents of her lashes, dark and feathery against her pink cheeks. Her rosy lips were parted, her breathing slow and steady and he felt a twist of something unknown deep inside him.

She was so damned…*unexpected*.

He swallowed.

She had surprised him the first time around with her innocence and she had surprised him this time by being so gloriously accessible. Her body had opened up with a delicious familiarity. It was as if she instinctively knew what pleased him—as if they had been designed to fit together perfectly.

What was the *matter* with him? Almost imperceptibly he shook his head, trying to clear the thoughts which had obviously been skewed by the heady cocktail of hormones which were surging through his bloodstream. But the movement must have woken her, because Hollie's lashes fluttered open and Maximo found himself dazzled by the light shining from her wide grey eyes. He saw a flicker of confusion cross her face, as if she couldn't quite work out where she was, or who with—and then her lips curved into a smile which only made him want to kiss her.

'Happy Christmas!' she said.

'And to you,' he said, his swift smile intended to inform her that he hadn't had a complete personality change during the night. 'Hollie—'

'It's okay,' she said quickly, before moving away from him towards the other side of the bed. 'You don't have to say a word. I know the score.'

'You do?' he questioned.

Hollie couldn't miss the look of surprise which had darkened his features. Was he worried she was about to start planning some sort of future with him, just because they'd had amazing sex? Was he so arrogant as to imagine that a long night of lovemaking had turned her head?

And wasn't he right to think that way when her heart was full of wonder at the beauty of what had happened? But Maximo would never know that. Not now and not ever—because if he did, it would destroy this fragile relationship of theirs.

'Of course I do,' she answered, her staunch words

helping disguise the distracting flutter of her emotions. 'We've already had the discussion. You don't want to be involved with family life and I'm cool with that, for all the reasons I gave before. Nothing has changed. I enjoyed last night and I hope you did too—'

'You know damned well I did,' he growled.

'Well, then.' She raised her eyebrows. 'What's not to like? Has the snow melted? Because if so, I can be on my way and out of your hair.'

Jumping out of bed, she grabbed the nearest velvet throw—which just happened to be scarlet—and wrapped it around herself, before padding over to the window, aware of Maximo's gaze burning into her, watching every move she made.

Part of her wondered if it had all been a dream and the snow nothing but a figment of her imagination. Hadn't she feared that this morning she would look out onto the dull greys and browns of a midwinter garden? But the scene which greeted her was as frozen and as beautiful as it had been the day before. A completely impenetrable world of white. Deep down Hollie knew it would probably be best for everyone if she could make her escape, but she couldn't help the sudden leap of her heart when she realised that wasn't going to be possible. Who could blame her for wanting to eke out this sensual liaison for as long as possible? 'Oh, dear.'

'Oh, dear what?'

'Bad news, I'm afraid. There's no sign of any thaw and it looks like there might even have been a fresh fall during the night. The road out of here is blocked, all right.' She turned back to face him, wondering what had caused his face to darken like that. 'Looks like my departure is going to have to be delayed.'

'You sound almost *disappointed*, Hollie. Are you so eager to get away?'

Hollie gave him the benefit of her brightest smile. Perhaps she was better at acting than she'd thought. Maybe her relationship with Maximo— if you could call it a relationship—was a bit like Christmas. There was all this amazing stuff on the surface, which made you feel fantastic at the time, but after a day or two it was all over, as if it had never happened.

And thinking of Christmas… Hollie sucked in a breath. Just because Maximo had set himself up as some kind of modern-day Scrooge, didn't mean she had to copy him, did it? They might not have a tree, or fancy baubles, but wasn't *adaptable* her middle name? She knew what the score was, which meant that she didn't have to try to impress him. She could just be herself, which she knew from some of her girlfriends wasn't always the case when you were with a man. Wasn't that a liberation of sorts?

So she shot him another smile. 'The only disappointment would be if we weren't going to celebrate Christmas, but that's not going to happen.'

'It isn't?' he questioned, with a frown.

'Certainly not.'

'But there's nothing here. The castle doesn't run to fairy lights,' he said sarcastically. 'And I told you. I don't like Christmas.'

'Maybe you don't, but I do. There's no need for us to forgo the festivities, just because we're lacking a few resources—and I don't intend to. Just leave it to me.'

The darkness in his eyes had been replaced by a sudden smokiness which Hollie recognised and it was with a feeling of falling—or failing—that she felt her body's instant response.

'I don't care about the damned festivities,' he ground out. 'All I care about is having you back in my bed again. Now come over here, Hollie Walker, before I lose patience.'

Hollie had never been quite so aware of her own power and for a few brief moments she revelled in it. 'Why don't you come and get me?' she said.

CHAPTER EIGHT

'Okay. You can open them now.'

The soft hands which had been covering his eyes were removed and Maximo grew still as he stared at the scene in front of him, unable to believe what he was seeing. He shook his head a little, but nothing altered. What the hell had happened? The previously bare room now seemed like a distant memory, replaced by a glittering and shimmering spectacle. Because Hollie had decorated the long table in the castle library for a late Christmas lunch. No. She'd done much more than that. She had actually decorated the whole damned room so that it resembled something you might see on the movie channel throughout the month of December.

Gleaming silver discs and squares hung from the ceiling, suspended by almost invisible pieces of thread. More dangled from a large branch of conifer, which somehow managed to resemble a miniature Christmas tree. And there were sprigs of holly just about everywhere—lying on empty book-shelves and decorously placed on the mantelpiece—plus an enormous bunch which had been stuck into a pottery jug as a centrepiece for the table.

As for the table…

Maximo been entertained many times during his life with no expense spared, because when a woman made you dinner, she seemed to think she was auditioning for a permanent role in your life.

But this was different.

He narrowed his eyes. Echoing the bright holly berries, the table was spread with what looked like the scarlet velvet throw which had adorned her naked body that very morning. Matching red rib-bons were tied in festive bows around two snowy linen napkins and everywhere there were candles. Tall candles and squat candles. Some which were near the end of their natural life and others which were clearly brand-new. Their flames flickered up-wards and wove intricate shadows against the walls, while more flames came from the fire which was burning brightly in the grate. His gaze moved to the window where outside dusk was falling on the pristine snowy scene, and the contrast with the il-luminated interior of the ancient room made the place look almost…magical.

'What have you done?' he husked.

She shrugged. 'I played around with what we had. The candles I found in the scullery. The shiny things hanging from the ceiling are cardboard, covered with silver foil which I discovered in a drawer in the kitchen—and the cotton comes from a sewing kit in my handbag. The napkins were in those hampers you ordered, as were the ribbons—and I found the rest of the stuff in the garden.' She chewed on her lip, anxiety suddenly creasing her brow. 'You do like it?'

'It's…it's a surprise,' he admitted at last. 'It's… well, it's remarkable.'

She looked at him a little uncertainly, as if unsure whether or not that was a compliment. 'Why don't you sit down?' she suggested. 'And I'll bring the food in.'

'I'll help.'

'No,' she said firmly. 'You won't. Humour me, Maximo. You waited on me at dinner last night and now it's my turn. I'm perfectly capable of carrying a dish or two. You can open the wine if you like and pour yourself a glass. I'm just having water— obviously. So let me go and fetch the food.'

Maximo uncorked the bottle and walked across to the fire to hurl an applewood log onto the already crackling blaze, more to distract himself from the spiky carousel of his thoughts than for any other reason. *This* was the reason he always turned down every damn Christmas invitation which ever came his way, because this kind of homely festivity mocked him. Every single time. It reminded him of the lives of others and all the things he'd never had. It made him think of families who cooked and ate together, laughing and talking as they sat around the table. And his discomfort was amplified by Hollie's presence, by her newly discovered sexuality coupled with the fact that she was pregnant with his child.

She returned to the room, carrying a large tray which he took from her, waving away her protests, and he watched while she left for a final journey to the kitchen. Her hips were swaying in unconscious invitation, and she looked almost unbearably sexy in a borrowed sweater of his, which came down to mid-thigh. When he had finally released her from his bed that morning she had bemoaned aloud the fact that she didn't have a change of knickers.

'Then don't wear any.'

'I can't do that!'

'Why not?' His query had been casual, but his heart had been racing like a schoolboy's. And she had looked at him, and he at her, and somehow their getting up had been delayed even further. She had straddled him with abandon and afterwards they had shared a bath and stayed there until their fingertips were wrinkled, and she had squealed with delight when he'd wrapped her in a bathrobe and carried her back into the bedroom.

He couldn't remember ever feeling quite so turned on by a woman and if she hadn't gone to so much trouble with the meal, he might have suggested they postpone it in favour of a far more sensual feast.

But Maximo couldn't shake off a lingering sense of disconnect as he sat down at the table. Because for some reason it felt as if ghosts were joining them and sitting at those empty chairs. The ghost of his mother, so recently dead. His father, too—though he'd only discovered his demise by reading about it in one of the national Spanish newspapers last year. He thought of Christmases past. He stared at Hollie's belly. Of Christmases future.

'There's some of your Cantabrian mountain stew, which I've reheated,' she was saying, shattering his troubled thoughts with her soft English chatter. 'And lots of lovely cheeses and meats from those fancy hampers. Shall I cut you a slice of this Iberico ham, Maximo?'

His tongue felt as if it wouldn't work, as if it were too big for his mouth. He shook his head, taking a sip of wine. Rich, red wine which warmed the blood like soup. He always drank this particular vintage during his preferred solitary Christmases, but tonight, he might as well have been drinking vinegar. Why was he so beset with the past tonight? he wondered with irritation—as if it were a heavy mantle around his shoulders which he couldn't shake off?

'Is something wrong?' she said as he put the barely touched glass down.

He shook his head. 'No, nothing's wrong.'

'Forgive me for contradicting you, Maximo, but something clearly *is*.'

'Let's eat,' he growled. Remembering that they'd missed breakfast, he forced himself to work his way through some of the food, though he noticed that Hollie was tucking into her own meal with a healthy appetite and, on some level, that pleased him. Eventually, she looked up from her plate of cheese and crackers, putting her knife down with a thoughtful expression on her face.

'You know, something has been puzzling me,' she observed slowly.

'Really?' he questioned, injecting a deliberate note of boredom into his voice because her analytical tone suggested she was intending to take the conversation somewhere he didn't want it to go.

'Any ideas?' she ventured.

'I have many attributes, Hollie,' he drawled, 'but mind-reading has never been one of them.'

But his sarcasm didn't deter her. She simply dabbed at the corners of her mouth with her napkin.

'When you told me about how you started in business, about breaking up big rocks in the road, there was something you failed to mention.'

'There were probably plenty of things I didn't mention.'

'Your parents, for one,' she said.

'Maybe that was a deliberate omission.'

'I mean, how did that happen?' she mused, as if he hadn't spoken. 'Because fourteen *is* very young, no matter how old you looked. You haven't explained what your parents had to say about you joining a construction team and working the roads.'

There was a pause. A pause which seemed to last for ever, giving him time to fall back on his familiar strategies for avoiding scrutiny. But something stopped him and he didn't know what. Was it the clearness of her grey eyes—or an expression of something like compassion which had softened her lovely face, rather than judgement? Almost as if she had guessed at the truth. He thought about what she'd told him about her own father—about his failure to be there for her. Maybe he and Hollie Walker had a lot more in common than he'd previously thought, and was it really such a big deal for the mother of his baby to discover a few truths about him?

'They didn't know,' he said.

'But they must have known. How could they not?'

'By that time in my life, my mother and I were estranged—'

'At *fourteen*?'

'Yes, Hollie. At fourteen. It happens.'

'And your father?'

He shrugged. 'He did not really deserve that title, for I only ever had the briefest of relationships with him.'

'Why?' she questioned quietly. 'What happened?'

His mouth tightened because this was the part which was definitely off-limits. The part he had taken extra care to filter from his life and online presence—confident in the knowledge that nobody else in the picture would disclose it, because it didn't reflect well on them. Very few people knew who his father had been, and that had always suited him just fine.

Yet suddenly he remembered the nurses who had looked at him so contemptuously when he had stood by his mother's deathbed all those weeks ago. Was it that which made him want to break the habit of a lifetime and unburden himself to Hollie? Those nuns who had judged him and found him wanting for his seeming neglect. His mouth hardened. As if anyone who was old and a mother was automatically some kind of saint who deserved unconditional love from her child—a child she had shunned and rejected.

'My mother was never married to my father,' he said baldly. 'I was illegitimate. Not such a big deal now, but pretty big at the time, particularly in the part of the world where I grew up.' He saw her flinch and wondered if she was thinking about her own situation, wondering whether she too would be judged in this small part of Devon which was now her home. 'My father was one of Spain's wealthiest men. Have you heard of the clothes chain Estilo?' he questioned suddenly.

'Yes, of course I have. Practically every woman on the planet has an Estilo piece in her wardrobe.'

'He owned it,' he said and saw her eyes widen in shock. 'He was married, of course. He had any number of lovers—my mother being just one of them.'

'And was she…content with that?'

His narrowed his eyes. 'No woman is ever truly content with being a mistress, Hollie. Maybe that's why she became pregnant.'

'With you?'

He nodded. '*Sí.* With me. He had told her from the very start that he wanted no children, for he already had two daughters—and although he desperately wanted a son, he planned to conceive one with his similarly aristocratic wife. Outwardly, his life was a model of respectability and he had no intention of altering that state. When my mother went to him with news I was on the way, I think she was expecting him to change his mind and divorce his wife, but he didn't. He didn't want the scandal or the damage to his reputation as a family man. So he ordered her from the house and gave her nothing, not even after I was born.' His mouth thinned. 'There was no acknowledgement that I was his child and certainly no maintenance.'

'But…if he was so rich—'

'To have compensated her would have been an

admission of liability and that was something he wasn't prepared to do.'

'She didn't go to the papers?'

'Like I said, it was a different world back then and he had most of the media in his pocket anyway.' His mouth hardened. 'So I lived from hand to mouth with a mother who was increasingly resentful that I had ruined her chances of having a "normal" life. Because where we lived, a woman who had a child out of wedlock was shunned.'

Her grey gaze was steady as she flicked her tongue over her lips. 'What happened?' she whispered.

He shrugged. 'My father had no other son and then his wife died and, behind the scenes, my mother was concocting a plan. I only learned afterwards that she had gone to his home and confronted him. Told him I looked exactly like him—which was true—and that I had his mannerisms. In the extremely macho world in which he operated, she appealed to both his ego and his pride. She asked would he not prefer his only son to inherit his valuable business, rather than his daughters—two women who would be bound to go off and have families of their own. So he agreed to give me a home in his enormous mansion in the centre of Madrid.' He smiled bitterly. 'I guess you might describe it as a trial run. Like taking on an apprentice on a temporary basis, to see whether or not they fit in. To see if I was suitable to be recognised as his son.'

'And what did you do?' she questioned, when the silence which followed his disclosure became elongated. 'Did you go?'

'Life at home wasn't exactly wonderful and I can't pretend that the thought of inheriting one of Spain's most profitable companies didn't appeal to a boy who had known nothing but hardship. So I went to my father's house...' He shrugged as his voice tailed off. 'And quickly realised that the situation I found myself in was untenable.'

'How so?' she whispered.

He was lost now. Lost in the dark memories of the past. He remembered being bemused by the amount of cutlery beside his plate, and cramming food in his mouth as if he were a street urchin. Which was exactly how he had felt. Like a poor boy who had wandered into a parallel universe. He remembered being amazed at marble-decked bathrooms the size of ballrooms and lavish dinners which could have fed a whole village. His stepsisters laughing because he didn't know which knife to use. The servants looking at him with a scorn they hadn't bothered to hide, as if recognising that he was an outsider. *Un bastardo.* And that was never going to change—he'd recognised that instantly. He'd stuck it out for as long as he could but it had felt as if he were trapped inside his own private hell.

'I wasn't made to feel *welcome*,' he summarised acidly and although she looked as if she wanted him to elaborate, he was damned if he was going to do that, for any frailties he possessed, he showed to no one. Nobody would ever see him vulnerable—not even the mother of his child. 'As dawn broke on Christmas Eve, I left to return to my mother and managed to hitch rides from Madrid to A Coruña. I arrived not long before midnight when the night was bitterly cold and the snow was falling. I remember seeing the Belen in the town square…the traditional nativity scene,' he elaborated, when he saw her frown. 'I thought my mother might be out— although I certainly didn't think she'd be on her way to Mass. She was more likely to be drinking in a bar.' He gave a short laugh. 'But she'd gone.'

'Gone?' she echoed. 'Gone where?'

'I never found out. She had cleared out all her stuff the month before and left no word or forwarding address.' It shouldn't have come as a shock, but it did. Because deep down he had always believed that she loved him, because she was his mother. But she did not love him. She never had. He had fallen to his knees in the icy snow and wept and that was the last time he had ever wept. At least he'd had food in his rucksack—the only thing he had taken from his father's house. And then he had begun to walk, though he didn't know where. He had walked on through the night and on Christmas morning he had stumbled across the construction site and waited there for workers to return after the Christmas break. And he had vowed there and then that he would never let anyone close enough to hurt him again.

'She wiped me from her life as if I had never existed,' he continued, the words falling from his mouth like stones. 'It was only much later, when I had started to make money, that she contacted me again.'

'And were you ever…reconciled?'

'We met,' he said tersely, staring down at his fingernails. 'But her main focus was on what I could buy for her, rather than making up for all those lost years. I provided for her throughout the rest of her life but I never saw her again until a couple of months ago.'

'She…died?'

He looked up at her, feeling himself tense up. 'How the hell did you know that?' he demanded.

'Something in your face as you said it. I could see your pain.' Her voice was soft again. How did she make it so damned soft? 'I'm sorry for your loss, Maximo. I know she was cruel to you, but she was still your mother.'

He wanted to deny that he felt anything but she was getting up from the table and walking round to where he sat, sliding onto his lap to face him, one bare leg on either side of his. She looked at him for a long moment before resting her head on his in an age-old gesture which had never come his way before. Maybe he'd never needed it before. It had nothing to do with sex—and everything to do with comfort. And it was powerful, he realised. Unbelievably... powerful.

He wanted to shrug her off, to tell her he didn't need any clumsy attempts at sympathy—but the words remained unspoken, the gesture never made. He could smell her clean, soapy scent and right then she seemed to embody all the virtues he'd never really associated with the women in his life.

Innocence.

Decency.

Kindness.

Suddenly a tension which had been coiled so tightly inside him started unravelling, like a line spinning wildly from the fisherman's rod. Something he hadn't even realised had been stretched to breaking point now snapped and he held her tightly, losing himself in an embrace so close that you couldn't have fitted a hair between them.

He told himself it was desire.

Because it *was* desire. What else could it be? The powerful beat of his heart and the low clench of heat were familiar enough, but his urgent need to possess her was off the scale. With one hand he hooked the back of her neck and brought her face down to his, revelling in that first sweet taste of her lips as her satiny hair spilled over his hands. He deepened the kiss and deepened it still more, until she was writhing around on his lap—her lack of panties instantly apparent from the syrupy wetness which was seeping into his jeans.

'Unzip me,' he urged throatily.

Instantly, she complied, although her fingers were trembling and it took some careful manoeuvring before he was free, and then at last he lowered her down onto his aching shaft, a ragged groan escaping from his lips as he filled her.

She rode him. She rode him as if she had been born to do just that. Was it instinct which made her so proficient at that age-old rhythm? Because it certainly wasn't experience. Yet she seemed to read him so well. As if she knew exactly when he wanted her to pull the borrowed sweater over her head so that he could drink in every second of her partial striptease and the luscious bounce of her breasts. She shook her hair, so that it moved around her bare shoulders like a shiny ripple of wheat. And then he was coming and so was she. Coming and coming and coming…and it was like no orgasm he'd ever experienced.

His shout of exclamation—or was it exultation?—was harsh. Imprecise. His body bucked helplessly beneath her. And when it was over she didn't say a word, and he was glad. He didn't want her attempting to give meaning to what had just taken place. Because it had no meaning. It was just a manifestation of their extraordinary physical chemistry.

He stirred, wanting to put a little distance between them. Needing space to order his befuddled thoughts. 'Don't you think maybe it's time for dessert?'

'But there isn't…' Her breath was warm against his neck, her words soporific and slightly slurred. 'I'm afraid there isn't any dessert.'

He pulled back from her and frowned. 'Really? I thought you brought cake with you?'

Unwillingly stirred from her sleepy state, Hollie stared back at him in confusion, suddenly remembering the wretched cake which Janette had insisted on commissioning. 'You really want cake now?'

'Why not?'

Why *not*? She hadn't wanted to present it to him at the time and she was even less inclined to do so now, because it seemed to symbolise some of the things which had been so out of kilter between them. It reminded her of the speed with which he'd left her bed and the way he'd distanced himself afterwards. Worst of all was the memory of his reaction to her pregnancy when he'd been so angry and cold. And she was slightly irritated that he'd asked for it now, because it was hardly the most romantic way to end what had just been the most erotic encounter of her life. But Maximo doesn't do romance, she reminded herself fiercely. He does sex. And that's all he does. Better think about that before you start fabricating any more foolish dreams about him.

'Of course. How could I have forgotten? I'll go and fetch it,' she said, sliding from his lap and plucking his sweater from the floor, before wriggling it over her head. After a detour to the bathroom she hunted down the cake, and when she walked back into the library, she found Maximo still sitting at the table, seemingly lost in thought as he stared across the room at the crackling fire. He looked up as she put the cake on the table, but his expression was shadowed and indecipherable— their mood of lazy sensuality seemingly broken. She wanted to cut him a slice before he had seen it, but he had risen from his seat to look over her shoulder, at the Spanish word for congratulations, which she had laboriously piped onto the white icing.

'"*Felicidades*",' he read slowly, and then pointed to a fuzzy-looking shape beside the word. 'And what's this?'

Did he guess it was a teardrop, which had fallen straight onto the coloured icing at a critical moment? Yesterday she might have concocted some flimsy excuse and told him that she'd been trying to create a star, but not today. Because he had told her stuff. He'd confided in her. Hard, painful stuff. He'd let his guard down, presumably because he'd felt as if, on some level, he could trust her. So maybe she should trust him, too. And besides, it wasn't as if they had any shared illusions about the future which could be tarnished by the truth, was it?

'It was a tear,' she admitted, meeting the seeking expression in his black eyes with a shrug. 'I was feeling a bit sorry for myself.'

'But you're not now?'

'No, I'm not. There's no point. If life gives you lemons, you just have to make lemonade.'

Maximo took the slice she offered him, breaking off a fragment and putting it in his mouth so that it melted in a sugary rush against his tongue. He thought about the days which had led up to this moment, and the days which would follow. His mind began to compose an agenda, just like when he took on a new business deal and had to deal with facts methodically. Whatever happened he would support his child financially—in a way in which his own father had never supported him.

Just financially?

He stared across the table at Hollie, who was studiously picking frosting off her own piece of cake, though not actually eating any. And suddenly he realised that, despite all her outward simplicity, the package she presented was way more complex than he'd first imagined.

He had been the first man to have had sex with her. The only man. That shouldn't have meant anything but the truth was, it did. It made a primitive satisfaction pulse through his body. And although that realisation should have unsettled him, somehow it didn't because it had shone a light onto something else he'd only just realised.

Going forward, he didn't *want* her sleeping with other men. Just as he didn't want his child calling another man Papi. Maybe his attitude could be described as possession but could also be described as pragmatism. Because if the lack of a father had cast dark clouds over his life, hadn't she experienced something similar? And if that were the case, then wasn't it comparatively easy for them to do something about it, to spare their own child a similar kind of heartache?

'Marry me, Hollie.'

She looked up from her crumbled cake, her expression one of shock then confusion, as if she hadn't heard him properly. She knitted her brows together. 'What did you say?'

'I said, marry me, Hollie.'

'Is that an…order?'

'Does my method of asking offend you? Do you want me to pretend?' he demanded huskily. 'To go down on one knee with a ring-pull from a cola can and tell you I'll buy you a thirty-carat diamond ring when we hit the shops?'

'No, Maximo, I don't want you to pretend anything. I want you to tell me why you've suddenly come out with this extraordinary proposal.'

There was a pause. She'd told him she didn't want him to pretend, so he wouldn't. 'Because I think it's the only sensible solution to our dilemma.'

'*Dilemma?* Is that what you call it?'

'Don't try to gilt-edge a situation which neither of us ever intended to happen,' he said roughly. 'But instead, let's try to make the best of what we have. To make the lemonade, as you said. I don't want this child to grow up thinking his father didn't want him.'

'But you don't, do you?' she questioned baldly. 'Want him. Or her, for that matter.'

He shook his head. 'Now that the shock has worn off, I find that I do.'

'But that isn't enough to justify marriage, Maximo.'

'*No lo es*—I agree. And if it were someone else, I suspect I would not be having this conversation. But I find you easy company, Hollie, and that is rare—for my past relationships with women have not been easy. And believe me, our sexual chemistry is even more rare.'

'But…marriage,' she said. 'Isn't that a rather extreme solution?'

Her continued opposition rather than the instant capitulation he'd been anticipating only spurred Maximo on—because never did he feel quite so alive as when he was having to fight for something.

'I don't think I'll have a problem living with you. Plus my work takes me away a lot, which would give us both space. You will never have to worry about money. Ever. And that will still apply even if you find the situation intolerable and ask me for a divorce.'

He looked at her, his eyes cool and expectant, and Hollie felt the lurch of something she couldn't quite define. Or maybe she just didn't dare to. Because surely she should be feeling offended by his rather brutal words. Surely she shouldn't be excited about the thought of getting wed to a man who was clearly offering marriage out of some archaic form of *duty*? But she was. She couldn't help herself. She might try to talk herself out of her feelings by applying logic, but they were still her feelings.

The truth was that she found him easy company, too. And while she had no experience of sexual chemistry, she didn't imagine it was possible for that side of their relationship to get any better.

But the main thing to consider was her baby.

Their baby.

She touched her fingers to her belly and felt a little spark of hope flickering inside her. Didn't she owe it to this innocent life inside her to offer their child the best possible start in life? To not have to worry about spiralling childcare costs, or the fact that her baby had no contact with a single other blood relative than her. Hadn't she grown up that way and found it lonely and miserable? And Maximo had experienced that too—he'd effectively admitted it to her earlier.

Yet she didn't have a clue about what passed for normal behaviour in the world of this privileged billionaire. For all she knew, he might want what she believed was called an 'open' marriage and some instinct deep in her gut told her she would find that intolerable.

'What about fidelity?' she blurted out. 'Are you intending to be faithful to me?'

'I am and I will,' he said, his voice suddenly growing harsh. 'But I will also be truthful, Hollie. And if ever I meet a woman I desire more than you, then I will tell you so immediately and we will dissolve our marriage.'

It wasn't the answer she'd wanted, but she guessed it would have to do. Because although once again his words were brutal, at least they were true. She thought of the story he had told her and the bitter sadness she had seen in his eyes as he'd recounted it. Maximo had his vulnerabilities too, she realised, just like her. Couldn't they be there for each other—to reach out to each other in times of need—united against a sometimes cruel world?

So Hollie nodded as a sudden sense of calm filled her and the smile she gave him came straight from the heart. 'Then I will,' she said softly. 'I will marry you, Maximo.'

CHAPTER NINE

THE THAW SET in and it was as if the snow had never existed. As if it had all been nothing but a dream. As if Christmas Day and the four days which followed had never actually happened.

Except that they had. At the end of that delicious and sensual sojourn in the ancient castle Kastelloes, Maximo Diaz had asked Hollie Walker to marry him. And her future had changed in an instant. Her image of herself as a plucky but sometimes lonely single mother had crumbled away and instead she was having to get her head around the fact that soon she was going to be the wife of the sexy Spanish tycoon.

Maximo was still sleeping as she slipped silently from the bed, wrapping herself in velvet—green today—before staring out of the window. Water was dripping from branches, from bushes—drip-drip-drip. The dark turrets of the castle were no longer topped by a crown of white and nor did the bushes look like giant white stones. The magic had gone, she realised, a sudden whisper of apprehension prickling over her as she studied Maximo's tousled black head lying against the pillow and all her suppressed fears were suddenly given life.

Would he wake up and regret the resolution they'd come to at the end of Christmas Day, when—possibly affected by the emotional aftermath of the things he'd told her—he had asked her to be his wife? Perhaps it would be better if she gave him the opportunity to retract words he might have delivered too hastily, and she wondered if she could manage to do it in a way which meant that neither of them would lose face.

His lashes fluttered open—so dark against the silken olive of his skin—and mentally Hollie steeled herself against his beauty as he surveyed her through a shuttered gaze.

'The snow has melted,' she said baldly.

'That's good.'

'Good?'

'Sure. Unless you were planning to build a snowman. Don't you need a change of underwear, and don't we need to get to London? If the roads are clear, it means we can go.'

'London?' She looked at him blankly. 'You never said anything about London.'

'My jet is in an airfield on the outskirts of the city, Hollie.' His voice was soft but his words resolute. 'And I'm due back in Madrid for a New Year's party I've promised to attend under pain of death if I don't. As my future wife you'll be coming with me and there's no reason why you shouldn't move in straight away.'

She hadn't considered living in Madrid either. How stupid was that? 'But I thought…'

'What?' he prompted softly, throwing back the pile of velvet throws to rise from the bed like a magnificent dark and golden statue brought to life, before walking towards her. 'What did you think?'

'That I'd…' It was difficult to think of anything when he was standing so close and so naked. 'Well, I'll have to work out my notice for Janette.'

'Seriously?'

She nodded. 'Of course.'

He shrugged, his eyes shards of glittering jet. 'Even though I could easily arrange for one of my staff to take your place?'

His suggestion made her feel dispensable. As if her job and her old life were of no consequence. And even though it *was* a simple office job which anyone could probably do, and even though Hollie had often found Janette difficult, she had no intention of disappearing in a puff of smoke simply because a rich man was snapping his fingers. If she fell in with his autocratic wishes so readily, it wouldn't bode well for the rest of their lives, would it?

'I'm afraid I can't do that, Maximo,' she said. 'I can't possibly break my contract. I don't want to sneak away from Trescombe under a black cloud.'

His face darkened, as if her determination surprised and slightly irked him. 'I am loath to be apart from you, Hollie—perhaps I've become a little too used to having you in my bed,' he murmured. 'But obviously we can work round it. We'll just have to jet between the two places until you're free to move, if that's what you want.'

Of course it wasn't what she *wanted*. In a way, she was terrified of being apart from him. Terrified that their affair and his subsequent proposal would get diluted by distance and prove as insubstantial as the Christmas snow itself. If she worked out her notice there was the very real possibility that Maximo would change his mind and Hollie didn't want him to change his mind.

She wanted this. Him. The whole package.

She wanted to be his wife. She wanted him to be a father to their baby.

But if Maximo was going to get cold feet, then surely it was better if they discovered it now rather than later.

'The month will soon pass,' she said, with a certainty she didn't feel.

'You think so?' He sighed. 'Then I guess I must be patient—which is not an attribute I've ever particularly been known for. I suppose I must admire your loyalty to your employer, Hollie—but that's all we're going to say on the subject, because I'm taking you back to bed.'

Hollie was still glowing when Maximo's limousine made its way up the hill towards the castle, and she began to get an idea how smoothly the world worked when it was powered by wealth. Decisions which might have taken weeks to evolve were enacted almost before you'd finished making them. Life became seamless and also a little bit scary as she was driven to her cottage and instructed to pack only the things she couldn't bear to be without.

'But we're not leaving Trescombe completely, are we?' she questioned. 'I mean, it's not like we're cutting ties with the place completely. Because when you start renovating the castle—'

'Let's just concentrate on the essentials for now, shall we, Hollie?'

And although his words were a little clipped, Hollie couldn't deny how comforting it was to have someone else make the decisions. She felt the tension leave her body, realising this was the first time she'd ever had someone to lean on. She had cared for her mother and supported her emotionally when she'd gone to pieces, and then she had cared for herself when her mother had died. Why wouldn't she? Yet she couldn't deny how great it was to let someone else take responsibility for a change.

'Okay,' she said. 'I'll go and get my things to-gether. Would you like to come inside?'

'No. I'll wait here in the car. I have a few calls to make.'

It took her less than twenty minutes before Hollie rushed out of the door with her little suitcase, half imagining that the limousine might have disappeared in the interim, like Cinderella's fancy coach turning into a pumpkin. But, no, it was still there—and the six-year-old twin boys who lived in the house opposite were gazing at the shiny black livery as if Santa's reinvented sleigh had made a post-Christmas appearance. As the chauffeur shut the door behind her, Maximo lifted a narrow-eyed gaze from his computer and Hollie got the distinct feeling he had forgotten she was there.

Through towns decked with Christmas finery, they were driven at speed to London, where Maximo announced his intention to buy her a completely new wardrobe, so she could arrive in Madrid suitably clad.

Which left her wondering exactly what was the matter with the way she looked now.

She stared rather moodily at her well-polished brown leather boots before lifting her gaze to his. 'Because I'll let you down, I suppose?'

'It's not a question of letting me down. You look like a college student,' he informed her, almost gently, his fingertips whispering over her mane of hair. 'Which is undoubtedly a wildly sexy look, just not one which is particularly appropriate for my future wife. If you aren't dressed suitably it will make you self-conscious, for you will be mixing with women who will undoubtedly be wearing very costly clothes.'

'Gosh, you're making our future union sound like it's going to be fun, Maximo.'

He smiled then—a slow, sensual smile which curled over her skin like a wisp of smoke. 'Oh, I can offer you fun, Hollie. Be in no doubt about that. Now wipe that apprehensive look from your face and kiss me instead.'

And wasn't it crazy how his kiss had the power to dissolve every last doubt?

The limousine dropped them at an expensive-looking department store in central London with doormen who looked as if they had stepped straight out of a Victorian novel. And although the post-Christmas sales had just started and there were stampedes of people buying sequinned dresses and puddings which would shortly reach their sell-by dates, Hollie was assigned a personal shopper all to herself, though Maximo's insistence on accompanying her took her a little by surprise.

He watched as she paraded before him in a variety of outfits and the molten smoulder of his eyes when he approved a particular article of clothing was flattering, yes—but his attention quickly turned back to his computer, as though his work was more engrossing than anything else. Of course it was. He was just dressing her up like a doll so that she wouldn't disappoint him in front of all his rich friends.

But she couldn't deny that the exquisite garments felt wonderful against her skin—more than that, they made her look like someone she'd never believed she could be. Why, at certain angles she looked almost…pretty.

'I suppose you've taken lots of women shopping in the past like this?' she probed.

'Not a single one,' he admitted. 'But then, I've never asked anyone to marry me before either. Just as I have never been quite so much in physical thrall to a woman as I am to you. And so, to avoid unnecessary repetition of predictable questions, shall I simply assure you that having my full attention like this is not the way I usually operate? Does that put your mind at rest, as well as flattering your ego, Hollie?'

It did. It made her feel…*special*. It made her want to whistle a tune, to sing out loud at the top of her voice. She felt as if she could conquer the world.

And when the shopping expedition was concluded and they had eaten lunch in a hushed restaurant with thick white tablecloths and women who watched him with predatory eyes, Maximo dropped her back at the store, where she was whisked off to a basement spa which smelt faintly of sandalwood and tuberose. There she had her first ever bikini wax, a pedicure and make-up lesson, though she begged them to go easy on the mascara. Next, a sweet girl in a white uniform took her to the hair-dressing section to have a couple of inches snipped off her mane and some choppy layers added. And when it was all done, she stood in front of the full-length mirror in her new silk dress, with a shiny fall of hair shimmering around her shoulders, and her transformation seemed complete.

She didn't look like Hollie Walker any more.

Neither an uptight office girl nor a giddy Christmas elf stared back at her today.

She looked like an expensive glossy *stranger*.

And when Maximo came to collect her, he must have thought along similar lines because he appeared almost taken aback by her appearance.

'*Bien, bien, bien*—what have we here, *mia belleza*?' he mused, his black gaze travelling over every inch of her, before he slid onto the back seat of the car beside her.

'You don't like it?'

'I didn't say that.' His hand slid over her thigh, his fingers stroking over the navy silk. 'You look out of this world.'

'Like an alien, you mean?'

He laughed. 'No, not remotely like that. Why do you always put yourself down?'

'Perhaps I'm not used to compliments.'

'Then I shall have to make sure you get used to them. Like a beautiful woman at her peak, is that better? My only complaint is that there isn't time for me to prove just how much you have excited my senses, because we need to buy you a ring before the shop closes.'

'We don't really have to do that today, do we, Maximo? Haven't we shopped enough?'

'I'm afraid we do. I was given to understand that women can never have too much shopping, although maybe you're the exception to the rule,' he added drily. 'But tomorrow, we fly to Madrid and I intend that you should arrive there wearing the biggest diamond in the world.'

Hollie supposed it would be churlish to object to having 'the biggest diamond in the world' on the grounds that she was feeling increasingly detached from reality with all this high-end purchasing power. Yet wasn't this just another example of making sure she was 'good enough' to meet his wealthy friends?

She tried to shake off her insecurity as he took her to a darkened store somewhere near Hatton Garden, which didn't really look like a jeweller's from the outside, and he and the owner began speaking in a language she barely recognised as English. They spoke of *cushion* and *marquise* and *princess*, which she gathered were cuts of diamonds, though when she emerged from the store an hour later, it was with an enormous rock called a *round brilliant* dripping from her finger.

As they were leaving, she saw a woman in the street do a double take when she spotted the size of the jewel. But all Hollie could focus on was the sobering thought that the entire purchase had been conducted with zero emotion. There had been no joy on the face of her husband-to-be as he slipped the priceless ring on her finger—just a glimmer of quiet satisfaction in his eyes as the shop's owner informed him that he had just purchased the finest gem in his collection.

Because there *was* no emotion involved, Hollie reminded herself fiercely as they got into the waiting car. There might be mutual attraction and a determination to do the right thing by their baby, but this marriage was nothing but a solution to their *dilemma*, and she should forget that at her peril.

'So where are we going now?' she asked, slightly dazzled by the rainbow rays which sparkled on her left hand and wondering if she would have to remove it when she was cooking.

He glanced up from his phone, momentarily distracted. 'We'll spend tonight at the Granchester Hotel, for you must be tired after so much travelling?'

'A little,' she admitted.

'And tomorrow we head for the airfield where my jet is ready to fly us to Spain, because it's New Year's Eve and we have a big party to attend.'

'How big a party?' she said, suddenly nervous.

'Very big. The Spanish love to celebrate the start of the new year and since many of my friends will be gathered together in the same place, it means I can introduce you as my bride.' He glanced at his watch. 'We should arrive in Madrid in time for lunch.'

'And that's where you live? In Madrid?' It seemed crazy that soon she would marry him and she didn't actually *know*. There were so many things about him she didn't know.

'Yes, I have an apartment there, very close to the Retiro Park. I think you'll like it.'

Hollie felt dizzy. London for shopping. Madrid for lunch. And a massive New Year's Eve party with, no doubt, all the world's glitterati there. Was this going to be her life from now on? She supposed it was. Would she fit in? Or, even with all her fancy new clothes and hairstyle, would she still look like ordinary Hollie Walker who worked in an office and baked cakes on the side?

But Maximo had put his phone away and was circling his fingertip over the palm of her hand and making her tremble, and her eyelids were fluttering to a close as he leaned over to kiss her. And really, what more could she possibly want?

CHAPTER TEN

'AND THIS IS my housekeeper, Carmen. Anything you want—Carmen will be able to get for you.' Maximo's eyes glinted as he ushered Hollie inside. 'Within reason, of course.'

'Encantada de conocerte,' said Hollie, using one of the phrases her fiancé had taught her during the flight over from London that morning.

'I'm very pleased to meet you, too. I speak fluent English, by the way,' added Carmen, with a smile.

Hollie beamed. 'Thank goodness for that.'

'And congratulations on your engagement.' Carmen shot a brief smile in the direction of the knuckleduster diamond. 'The staff are all delighted for you and Señor Diaz.'

'I appreciate that, Carmen. And it's wonderful to be here.'

Carmen inclined her head. 'Welcome to your new home.'

'Thank you.' Hollie slid her tongue over her lips.

Her new home—a huge and contemporary pent-house apartment overlooking Madrid's beautiful Retiro Park. It was terrifyingly immaculate, with not a single thing out of place, and as she shook the middle-aged housekeeper's hand she wondered if it would ever actually feel like home for her. But at least she was feeling calmer than she had done on the journey here. Their one-night stay at the Granchester Hotel had been unforgettable. Hollie had never stayed anywhere quite so luxurious and they'd been given an incredible suite with reput-edly the best view over the London skyline, because Maximo was friends with the owner.

But butterfly nerves had been fluttering in her stomach as her fiancé's jet had touched down in Spain and they had been driven straight from the airfield to his apartment. It had been daunting at first, meeting his staff—Carmen, and a permanent cook as well as a daily cleaner. But they'd seemed very open and friendly, and genuinely pleased to meet her, and that gave Hollie a flare of hope.

I can do this, she thought.

I will do this.

'Would you like to see the rest of the apartment?' asked Maximo softly, once they were out of Carmen's earshot.

'Yes, please,' she said.

'And then, after lunch, I think it is time to intro-

duce you to the very important Spanish tradition
of the siesta.'

'*Maximo!*'

'You do realise that every time you whisper my
name like that, it only turns me on some more, so
you must never stop doing it? Now follow me and
I will show you your new home.'

Hollie nodded, trying to concentrate on her surroundings, wanting to like them more than first
impressions had suggested she might. Because although she was aware that she was in one of the
most prestigious parts of Madrid, her initial reaction to Maximo's apartment had been one of disappointment. It was so modern and so *functional*.
The spaces were vast and curiously impersonal,
even thought they housed some pretty stunning furniture and artworks. Huge canvases adorned the
giant walls and most of the furniture was dark, soft
leather and almost tauntingly masculine. In fact,
dark was the theme which predominated—apart
from an illuminated wine cellar, which looked more
like an art installation, a dining room which overlooked the city lights and a floodlit rectangular lap
pool on the sprawling terrace, where Maximo informed her he liked to swim every morning before
breakfast.

She tried to find the right words to say. Tried
to imagine herself living here with a baby, with
all these hard and gleaming surfaces. She thought

about smudged little fingerprints clouding the acres of polished glass. 'It's lovely,' she said politely.

'There are plenty of good restaurants nearby and an interesting mix of people.'

'Gorgeous,' she said obediently, using the same tone she used to project in the office when a prospective vendor would canvas her opinion about the house they were just about to market. It wasn't a question of not being honest, it was simply showing consideration for other people's feelings. Because Hollie knew how a person could form a huge emotional attachment to their home. What right did she have to tell Maximo that she thought his apartment was a hideous monument to brutalism, when clearly he loved it? In England they often said an Englishman's home was his castle, well, maybe it was the same for Spanish men.

Yet all she could think about was a *real* castle, back in Trescombe, where they had shared that magical Christmas and candlelight had flickered intriguing shadows across the bare stone walls. Yes, Kastelloes could be chilly and, yes, the grounds were untamed and some of the interiors were crumbling away. But at least it had heart and soul and an artistic symmetry which took her breath away. Perhaps Maximo would capitalise on all those assets when he turned it into a luxury hotel to add to his existing group. She couldn't wait to see what he would do with it.

'Hollie?'

Maximo's voice interrupted her reverie.

'Mmm…?' she said absently.

'Weren't we talking about a siesta?'

She looked up, meeting the narrowed glint in his black eyes, and her heart turned over and melted. Who cared about bricks and mortar when a man looked at you that way? Who cared about anything when he could make her senses sing without even touching her?

'I believe we were,' she agreed and her answering smile seemed to spur him into instant and very masterful action. But she liked it when he made that soft roaring sound at the back of his throat and then carried her into their bedroom like a victor, carrying his spoils.

She liked it a lot.

Maximo watched Hollie's breasts rise and fall in time with her steady, even breathing. Her gleaming golden-brown hair was spread out over the pillow, her cheeks were lightly brushed with roses and she looked…

He swallowed.

Not beautiful, no. Her nose was a little too big and her lips not quite full enough ever to fit that imprecise and elusive definition which women craved and most men sought.

She looked sexy and serene. In fact, very serene and *very* sexy.

Once again he felt the tightening of desire low in his belly.

She had just flicked her tongue over his body and made his large frame convulse with spasms of delight he'd thought were never going to end. And afterwards he had done the same to her. Given swift featherlight licks against the hidden honey at the top of her legs, until she had clutched his bare shoulders with flailing fingertips and cried out his name.

But his remembered satisfaction was tempered by a sudden flicker of apprehension. She was the most perfect lover he could have ever imagined, and there had been a fair number during his thirty-four years of bachelorhood. But Hollie was like no other woman he'd ever known before. She was sweet and uncomplicated and innocent.

And she was having his baby.

His *baby*.

Didn't that give her a particular power—the kind of power he had vowed no woman would ever wield over him again? He could feel a sudden tightness in his throat. He had never wanted a child of his own, reasoning that someone who had never experienced parental love would be incapable of demonstrating any himself. He'd been scared of falling short and hadn't wanted another child to endure what he had endured. Plus, he'd liked his freedom and the ability to do what he wanted, when he wanted.

But now?

Suddenly he felt the winds of change upon him, and a feeling of inevitability blowing in their wake. He could sense a very different world opening up before him and simple, straightforward Hollie at the beating centre of it.

Hollie.

Hollie who seemed so soft and vulnerable. Almost *too* soft. *Too* vulnerable. He wasn't used to a woman looking at him that way, all wide-eyed and wondering. His mouth hardened. He would protect her and their child for as long as he lived, yes. He would give her whatever she wanted—hadn't he told her so just an hour ago, when he had carried her into the bedroom and stripped that provocative lingerie from her delicious body? She would have security for her and their child for the rest of her life, and he would put money in a trust to ensure that his son or daughter's future was secure. But those were practical needs he was able to fulfil, because this was a practical marriage and nothing more. He had made that clear to her when he'd asked her to be his wife and maybe now it was time to remember it himself. He wouldn't let her think this relationship was going to become any deeper than it already was, because that was never going to happen. Far better she get used to reality, rather than having her hopes raised and then dashed by unrealistic expectations. In the short term, wasn't it better to be a little cruel in order to be kind?

He stroked his fingers over the silky flesh of her cheek. 'Hollie?'

At the sound of his voice she began to stir, opening her eyes to find him watching her, and, almost shyly, she smiled. 'That was…amazing,' she said softly.

'Mmm. It certainly was, but now we must move. The party will already be in full swing and they're expecting us. Everyone's going to want to meet my fiancée.'

She bit down on her bottom lip. 'Have you told them we're engaged?'

'Not yet.' He lifted her hand and the dazzle of the large diamond shot bright fire over her hand. 'We'll let this ring announce it for us, shall we?'

'I'm nervous, Maximo.'

'Why are you nervous?'

'What if they don't like me?'

'Why wouldn't they like you? Now go and get ready and I'll ask Carmen to serve us a glass of *casera* before we leave.'

Hollie nodded and made her way towards the bathroom as Maximo's words echoed inside her head. Why wouldn't they like you? he had asked— because he had no comprehension of what it was like to be her. His world was very different and was inhabited by very different people. Would they welcome an unsophisticated stranger like her into their midst, or would they wonder if Maximo had taken leave of his senses?

She turned on the power shower and let the warm water bounce off her skin, telling herself she mustn't catastrophise the evening before it had even begun. Maximo's staff had already welcomed her with open arms and there was no reason why his friends shouldn't do the same.

She was feeling much better by the time she emerged from the bathroom, to see Maximo already dressed in a dark evening suit—a delectable sight which made her heart twist with predictable longing. He was lounging back in one of the bedroom's dark leather armchairs and looked up from his phone when she entered, clad in nothing but a snowy bathrobe.

'I haven't a clue what to wear,' she said, rifling through the row of new clothes which someone must have hung neatly in the wardrobe while they were having lunch.

'Wear the black,' he said suddenly. 'And put your hair up.'

'I thought you liked it down.'

'In bed, certainly—but tonight, no. Stop frowning at me like that, Hollie. There's a reason.'

'Am I allowed to know what the reason is?'

'In time.' He smiled. 'Be patient, *mia belleza*.'

Hollie began to get ready, fixing her hair and pinning it in place. Half an hour later and she was ready, a loose chignon coiled against the back of her neck, the black silk dress skimming her knees, and a pair of strappy shoes adding extra height. As she leaned towards the mirror to apply a light coat of lip gloss, Maximo walked across the bedroom and placed a small box on the dressing table in front of her.

'Why don't you put these on?' he said.

'These' turned out to be two long and sparkling columns—a pair of exquisite diamond earrings—and she stared down at them in confusion.

'But you've already given me—'

'Put them on,' he emphasised softly. 'I bought them at the same time as we got your ring. It's your Christmas present, Hollie.'

'But…but I haven't given you anything!' she protested, surprised when he leant over and placed the palm of his hand over her still-flat belly and their eyes met in a silent moment, reflected in the mirror.

'Oh, but you have,' he contradicted softly. 'You have given me something money can never buy. My baby.' There was a pause as she was caught in the ebony spotlight of his gaze. 'Would it bother you if we announced it tonight? It would kill speculation and everyone is going to know about it sooner or later.'

Hollie didn't answer straight away. She wasn't

sure she agreed because it still felt very…private, as well as very new. Yet it wasn't as though it were a guilty secret, was it? It was nothing to feel *ashamed* about. And if she was surprised by Maximo's desire to tell people, she couldn't think of any reason why he shouldn't—she was past the danger zone, wasn't she? 'No, I don't mind,' she said.

He turned away then, but not before Hollie saw the flash of something unexpected in his black eyes. A look which was hard and dark and very macho.

Was it triumph?

Was that why she felt a faint flicker of foreboding to add to all the others which seemed to be building up inside her? But she forced herself to push away her fears, determined to count her blessings instead. Tomorrow was the first day of the new year and the man she was going to marry was the father of her baby. Wasn't that good enough to be going along with?

He took her to the drawing room, which was situated at the very top of the large house, where they sipped glasses of *casera*—a simple bubbly lemon concoction, which Maximo said was rarely drunk outside Spain and which Hollie found delicious. Afterwards they were driven to the west of the city, to an upmarket area called Pozuelo de Alarcón, where the party was being held. The house was large and modern and surrounded by enormous grounds, with clever lighting focussing on beautiful outdoor statues and surrounding shrubs. Coloured bulbs were looped through the branches of trees, and as the line of luxury cars progressed up the long drive Hollie could see people laughing and drinking through giant plate-glass windows. It looked just like a commercial and Hollie would have defied anyone not to have felt intimidated by it.

Did her shoulders stiffen with tension—was that why Maximo ran a reflective finger over her palm? 'Everything okay?' he verified.

'I'm still nervous,' she admitted.

'Don't be, *mia belleza*. Your innocence will be like a breath of fresh air.'

'Not so very innocent any more,' she reflected ruefully.

'Everyone has to lose their innocence some time.' He reached up and touched his fingertip against one of the diamond strands which dangled like a spill of stars from her ear. 'You know that at midnight we have a big tradition in this country?'

'Like the siesta, you mean?'

'In its way, *las doce uvas de la suerte* is as important as the siesta, *sí*—because, to the Spanish, all traditions are important.'

Hollie nodded, wondering if that was because he'd grown up without any real traditions of his own.

As had she.

'Everyone eats grapes at midnight on New Year's

Eve,' he said. 'One for each stroke of the hour—twelve grapes in all.'

'Why do you do that?'

'To bring us luck.' He smiled. 'Rare is the Spaniard who will poison his fate for the following year by failing to complete this simple task.'

'In England, we might be tempted to call that superstition.'

'Then I shall have to persuade you otherwise, won't I?' he said softly as the limousine slid to a silent halt, and she shivered as he whispered his fingertip over her thigh, as if to remind her of what delights lay in store for them later.

Heads turned as they walked into the party—where even the people serving drinks and canapés looked as if they had stepped from the pages of a fashion bible.

Please don't let me make a fool of myself, Hollie prayed.

There was a split-second pause and then conversation resumed as a tall and very handsome man extricated himself from a group of people and came over to greet them.

'Maximo,' he said. 'I'm glad you made it, though I confess to being a little surprised.' His black eyes gleamed with curiosity. 'Since the word is out that there are going to be a lot of very disappointed women here tonight.'

Hollie felt Maximo's fingertips touch the base of her spine.

'Javier, I'd like you to meet my fiancée, Hollie Walker. Hollie, this is Javier de Balboa, a very old friend of mine, who will probably do his best to cause mischief.'

'Pleased to meet you,' said Hollie, her hand straying to her cheek to push away a dangling strand of hair.

'So it *is* true,' breathed Javier, and Hollie knew she hadn't imagined the surprise which flickered in his dark eyes as he spotted the large diamond gleaming on her finger. 'Wow. I am delighted to meet the woman who has tamed this black-hearted rogue after so long. You *do* realise what you're taking on, don't you, Hollie?'

'I think so.'

Her tentative words made both men smile and suddenly Hollie felt a little more comfortable as she asked for a glass of *casera*.

'You won't have champagne?' asked Javier.

'Hollie's pregnant,' Maximo cut in.

'Ah. Of course she is. My congratulations to you both. In that case, I will have someone prepare you a *casera*.'

After he had gone, Hollie just stood very still for a moment, breathing deeply and trying to compose herself. What had Javier meant—*Of course she is*? That it was inconceivable the powerful bachelor

would be contemplating marriage unless he was
being shotgunned into it? And wasn't that the truth?
She could see people watching them and wondered
how they saw her. As an upstart who had managed
to get her claws into one of Spain's most eligible
bachelors? One who was clearly out of her depth,
despite her designer dress and the jewels which
hung from her finger and her ears?

Maximo turned to talk to someone and, although
a nearby couple were eager to chat to her, Hollie felt
strangely isolated. She watched as Maximo seemed
to command the attention of everyone in the room.
People were trying to get near him and she felt as
though she were melting into the shadows and gradually becoming invisible. She realised that for him
this was truly home, and always would be.

She did her best to join in with the lively party
but couldn't quite contain the nerves which were
growing inside her. She saw a huge dish of purple
grapes gleaming rather menacingly in a corner and
prayed she would be able to match everyone else in
the room—although eating twelve grapes in such a
short space of time did seem a big ask, particularly
of someone who was pregnant.

She glanced around the room, thinking that she'd
never seen so many stunning women congregated
in one place, and found herself remembering what
Maximo had once said. He'd told her that if ever he
met a woman he desired more than her he would tell

her immediately and their relationship would end. Looking around at the model-perfect array of females, she failed to see how that could *not* happen. Surely once the allure of their brand-new sex life wore off, wasn't it inevitable he would be tempted?

She wasn't much of a drinker but right then she would have given anything for a small glass of wine to help quell her spiralling nervousness, but of course she couldn't do that because she was expecting a baby.

And that was the only reason she was here.

All of a sudden Hollie felt as if she were adrift on a life raft, floating on a wide sea. Lost and all alone—despite the proud-featured man at her side who drew the gaze of every woman in the room.

CHAPTER ELEVEN

HER NIGHT WAS RESTLESS—her sleep broken by ill-defined dreams which somehow scared her—and when Hollie awoke it was to find that Maximo had gone. She sat up in bed and blinked, glancing around at the unfamiliar space of his vast Madrid bedroom. Gone where?

As if in answer to her thoughts he walked into the room, dressed in his habitual black and talking on the phone on what was clearly a work call. He palmed her a wave but continued talking in Spanish, obviously distracted—and when Hollie emerged from the bathroom he was still speaking. She walked over to the window and stared out but, despite the beautiful Retiro Park being so close, all she noticed were the buildings and busy roads. She kept telling herself the problem lay with *her* and not the famously beautiful city of Madrid, but that didn't alter her fundamental fear about whether she'd ever get used to living here after the quiet of Trescombe.

Maximo cut the call and walked over to the window to stand beside her. 'You're awake,' he murmured, snaking his arm around her waist, his thumb stroking a slow circle. 'I thought I'd let you sleep. It was a late night. Did you enjoy the party?'

'It was certainly very lively.'

'Who was that woman I saw you talking to?' he enquired, his fingers reaching up to comb through the tangle of her hair.

'Which one? I was talking to lots of people.'

'The one in the green dress. She had blonde hair, I think.'

'Oh. You mean Cristina.' Hollie smiled. It had been one of the highlights of a very challenging evening. An elegant woman had walked across the crowded room and given her a warm and friendly smile. More than that, she had seemed instantly understanding, telling Hollie that she had once been the newcomer at a similar, glittering party. 'It can be a little overwhelming at the beginning,' she had said softly. 'They are a wonderful but rather intimidating crowd. Just give them a chance.'

'Who is Cristina?' prompted Maximo, breaking into her thoughts.

'She owns a shop on the…' she frowned as she tried to remember '…the Calle de Serrano, and wants me to have lunch with her some time, so I gave her my number. I explained I was going back to England tomorrow to work out my notice, but said I could meet her at the end of the month.'

'Good, good,' he said, as he linked his fingers with hers and began to lead her back towards the bed. 'It's important for you to make new friends.'

'What…what are you doing, Maximo?' she questioned, as he laid her down on the mattress and then began to peel off his clothes with impatient fingers.

'What do you think I'm doing? I'm going to make love to you because I am aching to be inside you again.'

'B-but, you've only just got out of the shower.'

'Then I'll just have to get right back in it, won't I?'

She felt the silky collision of his flesh as their bodies collided and heard the deepening of his voice as he brushed his lips over hers.

'Do I taste good, *mia belleza*?'

'You do.' She shivered. 'You t-taste very good.'

His mouth moved to her neck, her belly and then—most daringly of all—between her legs and Hollie's eyes fluttered to a helpless close as she felt that first deliciously precise flick of his tongue. Pretty soon her body was clenching with the explosive pleasure which was now part of her daily life.

How could I have lived without this for so long? she thought dreamily as she lay cradled in his arms afterwards.

How could I have lived without *him*?

But that was a dangerous way to think. Especially when the next few days made her realise that something fundamental between them seemed to have shifted. At first she thought she was imagining it, but gradually she realised that, on some level, their relationship had changed. It was difficult to define but it was definitely there. All the closeness and banter they'd shared over Christmas seemed to have evaporated. It had become functional. She told herself not to keep analysing the situation, but couldn't seem to stop herself. Because despite the undeniable intimacy she felt whenever they were having sex, hadn't Maximo been noticeably more distant with her ever since they'd arrived in Madrid? Hadn't he been obsessed with his work in a way she hadn't witnessed before? He seemed to be out at the office most of the time and when she had questioned him about it, he hadn't been in the least bit contrite.

'Surely you must understand that I have to work, Hollie,' he had replied, with a shrug. 'I am the head of a very big organisation and a lot of people rely on me.'

'And when the baby arrives? What then? Will you still be working around the clock?'

'Who knows? It's possible.' His black eyes were clear and gleaming. 'I'm not going to make any promises I won't be able to keep, *querida*. I'm planning to do the best I can, but I don't know what form being a husband and a father will take. Is that fair?'

It might have been fair, but it wasn't what Hollie wanted to hear—and while his honesty was admirable, it failed to reassure her. It felt to her as if he had achieved what he had set out to achieve—by offering her marriage—and was now free to turn his attention to other things. Would she be expected to build her own separate life here—a life which touched his only in parts? It wasn't what she had envisaged when she had agreed to marry him...

And before she knew it, it was time to fly back to Devon to work out her notice—an intention she had proudly insisted on but was now beginning to regret. Surrounded by luxury, Hollie stared out of the window of his private jet, wondering if Maximo would be relieved to have the apartment to himself again now she'd left. He certainly hadn't given any indication that he was going to *miss* her. And even though he made love to her that morning, and afterwards held her trembling body very tight, she could never remember feeling quite so alone.

It was weird being back in England. Weird yet strangely comforting—like climbing into a warm bath at the end of a long working day. As the limousine purred along the high-hedged country lanes, Hollie realised that people knew her here in Trescombe. She belonged in this little town. When she stopped at the local store to buy some provisions, the owner did a double take before her face broke into a huge smile.

'It *is* you! Why, for a moment I didn't recognise you, Hollie!'

Hollie blushed, realising she hadn't even considered the impact of leaving a fancy car sitting on the kerb waiting, while she purchased her pint of milk wearing a whacking great diamond ring, and a cream cashmere coat which must have been achingly expensive.

She would need to go back to her trusty skirts and blouses tomorrow morning when she started back at work. Her mind flitted over different possibilities as she wondered how she was going to explain what had happened to Janette. Was she going to give her boss the whole story, chapter and verse, and tell her she was engaged and pregnant in a single sentence?

Her boss was so...probing. She would almost certainly pry and ask Hollie what it was like being engaged to someone as charismatic as Maximo Diaz. She might even ask her details about how it had happened.

And Hollie would say—what?

That it had been a one-night stand with far-reaching ramifications, hence the Spanish tycoon's shock proposal of marriage? She certainly wasn't going to hint at her growing insecurities about her place in Maximo's life or confess that he seemed to be pushing her away from him. Hollie bit her lip. He'd made it clear he didn't want deep, or mushy, or lovey-dovey from their relationship—yet despite knowing those things, it made little difference to the way she felt about him. She still felt dizzy with longing whenever she thought about him.

Perhaps it was the thought of how it had been before which kept her snared—all those evocative memories of a snowed-in Christmas, which had led her to believe in all kinds of possibilities. The way he'd taken her into his confidence and the way he made her feel when she was in his arms... Perhaps it was her lack of experience of sex which made her ultra-susceptible to its influence. Because sometimes, when she was lying close to him, with the powerful beat of his powerful heart slowing in perfect time with her own, Hollie would feel something close to...

Love?

She swallowed. Was it possible to love someone even if you knew that was the last thing they wanted from you?

Was it?

Yes, of course it was possible. People had been falling in love indiscriminately since the beginning of time. And, despite all her mixed-up feelings, Hollie's heart still lifted with joy when she answered Maximo's text asking whether she'd settled in and saying he'd call her later. His brief message made her think. It made her look at the situation from a different viewpoint. Back in Madrid she had convinced herself she was missing her simple life in Trescombe, but the irony was that she was missing Maximo a lot more. Didn't she ache for him with a fierce longing which was almost visceral? And if that was the case, then surely fitting into her new world in Spain wasn't only preferable, but achievable. All she had to do was to give it a decent chance, and that meant giving it time. Couldn't she choose her moment to suggest that he didn't have to work quite so hard—and couldn't they get back the kind of closeness they'd had before?

Feeling suddenly light-hearted, she made herself a sandwich and sat down at the table munching it as she looked around. Her little pine tree was wilting and had deposited most of its needles onto the rug, and two of the baubles had fallen to the floor. Christmas really was over and she was going to have to think about taking all these decorations down before Twelfth Night.

She was just about to leave for work next morning, when she heard her phone vibrate and she slid it out of her handbag to look at it.

It was a number she didn't recognise. An international number—Spanish, she thought. And when she clicked on the call she discovered it was Cristina, the woman she'd met at Javier's party. The woman with the potential to be a new friend. The blonde in the green dress.

'Hi,' said Hollie, a smile entering her voice. 'How lovely to hear from you! How are you?'

'I'm…well. You have returned to England, I think?'

'That's right. I'm just about to go to work. I'm flying back at the beginning of February.'

Cristina's accented voice dipped by a fraction. 'And Maximo. Is he there with you?'

'No, I'm afraid he's not. He's coming over at the weekend.'

'I see.' There was a pause. 'I understand you're pregnant, Hollie? I really should have congratulated you at the party.'

'Yes, I am.' Hollie felt her heart give a little kick. 'I'm twelve weeks along. The scan is on Wednesday.'

There was another pause but this time, Cristina's voice sounded different. It quivered with the air of somebody who knew something. More specifically, who knew something you didn't.

'I like you, Hollie,' she said slowly. 'And I have learned something which is difficult for me to tell you, but which I feel you ought to know.'

'You're scaring me now,' said Hollie, only half joking. 'What is it?'

'It's about Maximo.' There was a pause. 'About the real reason he's marrying you.'

It was an extraordinary thing for someone to say

out of the blue like that—especially someone who didn't know you—and for a moment Hollie's only response was silence. Her fingers tightened around the handset and she could feel her throat constrict. She felt faintly disappointed. As if she had misjudged Cristina, who perhaps didn't want to be her friend at all. If she were a different kind of person she might have frostily retorted that it wasn't any of the other woman's business. But she wasn't going to hide from the truth, and if Cristina was expressing what everyone else was thinking, then maybe the subject would be better addressed head-on. 'I'm not naïve enough to believe the wedding would be happening if I weren't pregnant,' she said quietly.

'I'm sure you're not. But he's not just marrying you in order to maintain respectability,' Cristina said, and then the words came out in a rush, as if she was embarrassed to repeat them. 'He's marrying you because he stands to inherit the family business, which will be put in trust for your child. Only the will stipulates that the child must be born within wedlock.'

Hollie froze.

But Maximo had been estranged from his father since the age of fourteen. He'd told her that.

With her free hand, she gripped the back of a nearby chair. 'I don't believe you,' she whispered.

'I'm afraid it's true, my dear,' said Cristina. 'I heard this through Beatriz, one of his stepsisters. It was a hotly contested clause in the will, although the lawyers assured them it was watertight. They are obviously angry that their father's illegitimate son stands to inherit one of the most profitable companies in Spain. I'm sorry, Hollie. I felt it best you should know, but this is not news I would ever wish to be the bearer of.'

'No. Thank you.' Hollie's voice was brisk now. Polite, even. 'I appreciate it, Cristina.'

With a few more robotic words she cut the call, though all the time she was berating herself. How *stupid* she had been. Sorrow clamped its way around her heart like a vice and then she gave a bitter laugh. She might have lost her virginity but that didn't mean she wasn't still laughably naïve, did it? She had stupidly imagined she had no illusions about the opposite sex, but it seemed she was still capable of being blinded by the stars which had temporarily danced in front of her eyes. She had wanted love so badly that she had been prepared to overlook what was blazingly obvious. Because she didn't know Maximo at all, not really. The man she saw was the man she had wanted to see, not the one with hidden depths which he kept concealed from her. He was marrying her to gain control of one of Spain's most successful companies. Of course he was. Although he certainly didn't need the money, maybe he felt it was a justified legacy—to make up for his father's rejection. Payback time. But it didn't alter one key and painful fact…

That he had betrayed her, just as her father had betrayed her mother.

Her knees felt weak and she gripped the back of the chair even harder, afraid they might buckle. But the weirdest thing was that after that moment of dizziness had passed, Hollie felt calm. Icy calm. Almost as if she had been expecting this. As if things had always been too good to be true.

Because they were, weren't they?

Plenty of women got pregnant without getting married. Did she *really* think that someone like Maximo Diaz would ask someone like her to be his wife if he didn't stand to gain something from it, especially when he'd told her right from the start he didn't want a baby? Or had she walked into the self-deceptive trap of thinking they had something special between them, just because she'd fallen in love with him?

She had fallen in love with him.

Well, more fool her.

He stands to inherit the family business. Cristina's words were branded on Hollie's brain like fire.

If he'd told her himself, she might have understood. If he'd said *Look, this baby means that I can get something I've always lusted after*, she probably could have accepted it. If he'd kept it coldly businesslike from the beginning, then perhaps she wouldn't have built up all those fantasies in her head. But he hadn't and that had given her imagination a free rein. No wonder she thought she'd seen a look of triumph on his face when he'd asked if they could announce the pregnancy. He was probably rubbing his hands with glee at the thought of all that new power.

She picked up her phone, turning it over and over in her hand before finally tapping her fingers over the keypad. It took longer than it should have done but that was because her hands were trembling so much. She kept the message short—because, really, it all boiled down to one simple fact whichever way you looked at it.

Maximo…

A tear dripped onto the back of her hand and, impatiently, she shook it away before continuing to type.

Being back in Devon has given me a bit of time to reflect on things and I just don't think it's going to work out between us.

Her finger hovered as she battled between the desire to put as much distance between them as possible and the knowledge that she needed to act like a grown-up.

If you like we can talk in a couple of days. Hollie.

She didn't put any kisses, and that drove home the realisation that there had never been any of the stuff which defined most *normal* love affairs. No letters or texts of undying devotion. Just sex and a baby and a big diamond ring. She thought about the turrets and towers of Kastelloes and the thick snow which had trapped them there. She remembered how grateful she had been to that inclement weather, because it had brought her into Maximo's arms. She'd been blown away by her Spanish lover, and hopeful when he'd opened up his heart to her. The world had felt tinged with magic, when all the time…

All the time he had been using their marriage as a way of getting his hands on the family business.

What a trusting fool she had been.

Well, not any more.

She had once told Maximo that she could do all this on her own and she would—with or without his financial assistance. Because anything would be preferable to a lifetime of deceit.

She tugged the heavy ring from her finger and it clattered as she put it on the table and then, letting out a shuddered breath, she laid her face against her cradled arms and wept.

CHAPTER TWELVE

A THIN DRIZZLE of rain coated the windscreen in a slimy film as the car turned into the wintry English road. Maximo eased his foot off the accelerator, bringing the powerful vehicle almost to a halt so that it crept along at a snail's pace. He stared fixedly ahead, not caring if he was wasting time. Because he needed time to work out what he was going to do. To assemble his whirling thoughts into some sort of order before he saw Hollie.

To say what?

He still didn't know.

He thought about the bald little message he had received from her.

I just don't think it's going to work out between us...

He had been taken aback by the dark surge of pain which had flooded through him.

He had wanted to lift the phone and demand to

know what had made her write it, but something made him change his mind—though he didn't stop to think what that might be. Instead, he sought a solution in action, because that was how he operated. He had ordered his jet to be made ready and within hours had flown into Exeter airport, planning his movements with the precision of a cat burglar.

Unobserved, he had watched Hollie leave the office and a wave of relief had swamped him as he'd seen her familiar figure walking towards the bus stop. And although every part of him had ached to drive up and tell her to get in the car, he'd resisted the powerful temptation to do so, because he didn't want any kind of confrontation or public spectacle. He didn't want to run the risk of her refusing to travel with him.

He had seen the chill wind blowing at her hair, but the tresses were no longer unfettered and free as he liked them. They had been tamed beneath a hat he'd never seen her wear before, and the coat she was huddling into was not one of the items he had bought her, but a well-worn relic from her old wardrobe. It was as if she had embraced her old life and cut him out completely, he thought, and his heart gave another painful clench as he increased the speed of the car.

Once he had vowed never to let a woman close enough to hurt him. What had happened to that fervent vow from which he had never wavered? The vow he'd made on his knees on that snowy Christmas Eve in Spain, all those years ago.

You could leave now while there's still time, a cold and pragmatic voice in his head reminded him.

But he ignored it.

His car slid to a halt outside her tiny cottage and he crunched his way up the gravel path. Ignoring the twee little bell which dangled in the porch, he lifted his arm and began to pound on the door and the mighty sound created by his fist echoed through the still night air.

Someone was knocking at her door and Hollie paused in the middle of washing up her teacup. No, it was more like a pounding. The sound which someone who was in a hurry—or a temper—would make. Someone autocratic and powerful who wouldn't think twice about making enough noise to wake the dead.

Her throat dried. There was only one person she knew who would knock like that. Was that why her heart started racing as she put her teacup down and headed for the door? Or was it just that deep down she'd been expecting this visit and now the moment had arrived, she felt a terrible fatalistic sorrow washing over her?

Drawing in a deep breath, she pulled open the door and there stood Maximo. His hair was windswept and he was dressed in the black clothes which were so familiar, but Hollie had never seen that expression on his face before. It was tense. Brittle. As if he were holding something dark and unwanted inside him. His eyes narrowed, and then he spoke.

'Can I come in, please, Hollie?'

Did he really think she would refuse him entry? That she would *want* to? Because even though she recognised that the final minutes of their relationship were ticking away, Hollie wasn't feeling the things she wanted to feel. Despite the fact that he had used her as a pawn in his ambitious game plan, she wasn't hating him, or not fancying him. Her stupid stomach still turned to mush when he brushed past her, forcing her to shut the door on the drizzly evening outside.

For a minute she was tempted to throw herself into his arms in an effort to blot out all those things she'd discovered. Or even to ask if he'd like some coffee after his long journey, in a futile desire to put off the inevitable. To act as if she were still going to be his wife and make like they were going to be a happy family.

But she couldn't do that any more. She couldn't pretend—not to him—not even to herself.

Especially not to herself.

Uncharacteristically, he seemed almost hesitant as his gaze swept over her. 'Is the baby okay?'

Of *course* that would be his number one concern.

'Everything's fine,' she answered briskly. 'I'm having the scan the day after tomorrow.'

There was a pause, and now the light from his eyes was very hard and very bright. 'Do you want to tell me why you sent that text?'

Hollie tried to think of the right words but there were no right words. Only wrong ones. Harsh, discordant words which had the power to destroy everything and now she was going to have to say them out loud and make it all real.

'Do you want to tell me why you asked me to marry you, Maximo?' she questioned quietly. 'Only give me the *real* reason this time!'

His frown deepened. 'But you know the reason.'

'Yes, of course I do. Because of the baby. Or so I thought. We were supposed to be completely honest with each other, weren't we? We said that truth was going to define our relationship. Yet all the time...' She swallowed. 'All the time there was this great big secret bubbling away in the background, which you failed to mention.'

'What *secret*?' he echoed. 'You've completely lost me now.'

'Please don't treat me like an idiot!' she snapped.

'Then why don't you stop speaking in riddles? I told you. I don't know what you're talking about.'

'I'm talking about inheriting your father's business!'

He shook his head. 'Nope. Still confused.'

His words sounded genuine but Hollie steeled her heart against them, because men could lie, couldn't they? In fact, men *did* lie. Her father had rarely spoken a true word in his life, according to her mother.

'Cristina rang me up. The blonde in the green dress at the party,' she continued. 'She knows your stepsister, Beatriz.' She heard his sudden sharp intake of breath, which she interpreted as guilt.

'Beatriz,' he said slowly. 'Well, well, well. Now it really *does* get interesting.'

Hollie sucked in a ragged breath. 'Cristina told me about the will. About how your father left you controlling shares of his business, but only if you have a child born within wedlock. So why didn't you tell me that, Maximo? If you'd told me the truth in the first place then maybe I could have lived with it. It's the lies I can't stand.'

But there was no guilt or resignation on his face. No sense of having been found out. In fact, there was nothing on his sculpted features but a look of growing comprehension.

'This is all news to me, Hollie,' he said slowly. 'If there is such a bequest then it has never been on my radar, because I have been estranged from my family for many years and in all that time I haven't spoken to my stepsisters—not since they decided that cruelty towards an impressionable young boy was a sport they relished.' His voice harshened.

'Do you really think I would conceal something like that from you?'

'Yes! If you want the truth, yes, I do!'

Maximo flinched as if she had hit him, but through the slow burn of injustice came a powerful rush of feelings. Uncomfortable feelings he had buried for years and if it had been anyone else, he would have slammed his way out of there and taken his outraged pride with him.

But this wasn't just anyone. This was Hollie. Hollie who knew more about him than anyone else did. He remembered when he'd told her about working on the roads as a teenager and she'd asked him if he had lied about his age, as if it was important. As if it had meant something. Because it *did* mean something. She was used to men lying to her. Her father, for one. Did she think he was cast out of the same mould and that he would deceive her about something as big as this?

And then he wondered how he dared be such a hypocrite. Why *wouldn't* she believe that, when he had done nothing but push her away since she'd arrived in Spain, and maybe even before that? He had been so damned keen to create barriers between them and to ensure she knew never to dare cross them, that he had succeeded in destroying all the ease and the intimacy which had once existed between them. And now she was looking at him warily, with sadness and mistrust written all over her lovely face, and although he knew he deserved all of that—and more—suddenly he couldn't bear the thought that he might have sabotaged, not just his own future, but that of his family. *His family with her.*

'I repeat, I knew nothing about this legacy, and even if I did, do you really think I'd want his damned business? If I had, I might have stayed on in that heartless mansion—enduring the taunts of my stepsisters and the sniggers of the servants who surrounded him. Do you really think that even if I were poor—*even if I were poor*—I would accept the charity of someone who had never wanted me during his lifetime? Do you, Hollie?'

The fierceness of his tone must have convinced her, for she gave a brief and reluctant shrug. 'I guess not.'

But the wariness was still there and Maximo knew he had a long way to go. He could feel his jaw hardening—locking so tight he could scarcely grit the next words out, but then he'd had a whole lifetime of suppressing stuff instead of articulating it.

'I didn't lie to you about the will,' he said slowly. 'But in a way, I was lying to myself.'

Her eyes widened. 'What…what are you talking about?'

'I lied about the way you made me feel. I refused to acknowledge that you touched something deep inside me right from the start. And as that feeling

grew, it scared me. It made me feel…powerless—
and I had vowed that nobody was ever going to
make me feel that way again.' He expelled a long
and ragged breath. 'I thought when I took you to
Spain—that if I could get back to the way I normally felt, I could deal with it. I was stupid enough
and arrogant enough to believe I could just slot you
into your own little compartment in my life and you
would be content with that. But instead, I drove
you away—'

'Yes,' she said. 'You did.'

'I shouldn't have done that,' he ground out.

'No, you shouldn't.' She hesitated. 'But we all
say and do things we shouldn't, often because we're
scared. You're not the only one, Maximo.'

'Hollie—'

'No, wait.' Her firm tone belied the sudden
trembling of her lips and, suddenly, her voice was
trembling too. 'Let me confess something to you.
Something I'm only just starting to realise—which
is that I felt almost *relieved* when Cristina told me
about the will.'

'Relieved?' he verified incredulously.

She swallowed and nodded. 'Maybe it suited me
to believe that all men were fundamentally liars
and you could never trust any of them because that
way…' Her eyes had suddenly become very bright
and her words tailed off as she looked at him.

'That way you'd never get hurt?'

'Yes,' she whispered. '*Yes*. I didn't want to get hurt and I didn't want my baby—'

'Our baby.'

She bit her lip as if she was about to cry. 'I didn't want our baby to grow up the way I did,' she said huskily. 'In a world of broken promises and no real love. Or one-sided love. I thought it would be easier to go it alone than to do that. Because I want a *real* family, Maximo—not something which just looks like it from the outside—and I'm not going to accept anything less than that.'

This still sounded like bargaining to him and was not the instant capitulation Maximo had expected to hear. It still felt as if someone were squeezing his heart with their fist—and it hurt. It *really* hurt. He'd spent his whole life avoiding emotional pain and maybe that was why he had built up no resistance against it. Because suddenly he realised that if he wanted Hollie, he needed to really put his feelings on the line. To say things he'd never expected to hear himself say and make sure she knew he meant them.

'I've never told you that I love you, have I, Hollie?' he questioned unevenly. 'I've never told you that first time I lay with you, it felt as if you were touching me with flame? As if you'd unleashed the lick of a potent fire which threatened to melt the coldness deep inside me, which I'd lived with for so long? I'd never felt that way before and it made me feel vulnerable. That's what made me want to push you away.'

'Maximo—'

But he silenced her with a shake of his head because he couldn't allow her forgiving nature to let him off the hook. Not this time. 'You withstood my appalling attitude when I discovered you were pregnant—as if I had nothing to do with it!' He gave a bitter laugh. 'And then you created the kind of Christmas I'd never had and never thought I'd wanted, but it seems I did. For the first time in my life, I discovered what people meant when they talked about coming home. You are my home and I love you, Hollie, and I want to share my life with you and our baby.' He shrugged. 'It's as complicated and as simple as that.'

'Oh, Maximo,' she said, so quietly he could hardly hear her.

He opened his arms to her and she went straight into them, like a bird arriving back on the nest after a long flight away. She buried her head against his shoulder and he held her until she had stopped crying and then he turned her face up towards him, tracing his fingertip over the tracks of her tears. 'But I've been thinking about my bachelor apartment in Madrid and I've recognised it isn't really suitable for a baby,' he mused.

'But it's right next to that beautiful park.'

'*Sí*, it is, but I got the distinct feeling that you're

not much of a city girl, which was one of the reasons you left London, wasn't it?'

She shrugged. 'I guess.'

'When I took you there, I felt as if I had plucked
a wildflower from a country meadow and trans-
planted it into a hothouse. Which is why I'm planning to fit into *your* world from now on.'

Her brow creased into a frown. 'Now who's talking in riddles?'

'There's something else you need to know,' he
said suddenly. 'Something I should have told you a
whole lot sooner. I was never planning to turn the
castle into a luxury hotel. That was just an assumption local people made and I didn't bother to correct
them. I had planned to demolish it and turn it into
a quarry—to use the valuable stone it was built on
to build a railway track.'

'You…you were planning to destroy hundreds of
years of history just to build a railway?'

'Don't knock railways, Hollie, because we need
them—now more than ever.'

'Why didn't you say something before? Why
didn't you tell anyone?'

'Because I knew if that fact got out, it would
drive up the purchase price.'

She punched a half-hearted fist against his chest.
'That is the most hard-hearted thing I've—'

'I'm a businessman, Hollie,' he interrupted gently.
'And that's what businessmen do. I'd planned to stay

there over Christmas because I knew it would provide the solitude I was seeking, and then to sell it in the new year. I wasn't expecting to meet a woman in this one-horse town, and have my life turned upside down by her. You were the reason I couldn't go through with the sale, not when I saw how much the place meant to you. I realised I couldn't take a wrecking ball to the heart of this little community in order to steamroller another money-making scheme.'

'Oh, Maximo,' she said, lifting her left hand to her heart, making him notice she wasn't wearing her engagement ring.

'I have been thinking that we could keep the castle and turn it into our family home, if that's what you wanted. Or maybe turn it into a hotel and buy a big house and garden for our family instead, if that's what you'd prefer. I was waiting for the perfect moment to tell you, only perfect moments have a habit of being elusive. But those things could only happen...' His words tailed off and somehow he was finding it impossible to keep the sudden break from his voice. 'They could only happen if you still wanted me. If you still wanted to be my wife.'

Hollie put her arms around his neck and pressed her face very close to his as a powerful shaft of joy and gratitude shot through her. 'Of course I still want to be your wife. Because I love you,' she whispered. 'I love you in a way I never thought possible, but I never believed you might feel the same way about me.'

'Believe it now.'

'I do.' She looked into his black eyes and saw a look of true understanding, but she knew there was more to tell him. 'When I thought you'd lied to me, I took the coward's way out. I was trying to protect myself against hurt and pain. That's why I sent you that text instead of waiting until you got here and talking it out with you, face to face.'

'*Querida*—'

'No, let me finish.' That was easier said than done when tears were starting to stream down her cheeks—big and wet and salty and dripping on her sweater. 'But the worst hurt and pain I've ever experienced was imaging a life without you…' Once again her words tailed off and it took a couple of moments before she could catch her breath to speak. To articulate the emotion which Maximo had never been shown as a child and convince him that she meant every single word. They had both been damaged in the past, yes, but love was the true healer. Some might say the only healer. 'I love you with all my heart, Maximo Diaz,' she whispered. 'And I'll never stop loving you. Believe me when I tell you that, my darling.'

His slow smile was like the sun coming out and the glint in his eyes warmed Hollie's heart. And when he caught hold of her she felt as if she'd been reborn. As if he were breathing new life in her, to join the life which grew beneath her heart. Blindly, her lips sought his and as they kissed, the salt water of their mingled tears slowly began to dry.

EPILOGUE

'SLEEP IN HEAVENLY PEACE...'

The poignant last notes of the carol seemed to hover on the still night air as, fortified by a pitcher of mulled wine and a platter of home-made mince pies, the group of singers began to make their way down the hill towards the town. Hollie glanced up at the sky as several large, feathery icicles drifted against her cheek. The bright moon of last night was obscured by cloud as the first fat flakes of snow started falling. There should be a thick covering to-morrow, she thought with a glow of satisfaction, as she closed the door of her castle home.

In the wood-panelled hallway stood a tall fir tree, decked with plain white lights and tartan ribbons and topped with an organza-robed angel. There was another tree in the library, where tomorrow they would eat a late lunch, illuminated by as many candles as she could lay her hands on, as had now become a yearly festive tradition. Mistletoe dangled in the hallway and there were bunches of holly and fragrant green garlands strewn everywhere. In the kitchen, a large pot of Cantabrian mountain stew was quietly bubbling away—also a tradition. It was Christmas Eve and it was perfect.

'Will Father Christmas come tonight, Papi?' asked a little voice from behind her and Hollie turned around to see her sleepy son nestled snugly in his father's arms.

'*Sí*, he will come to visit every child in the world tonight,' murmured Maximo, meeting her gaze over Mateo's tousled black head. The smile he slanted her was full of promise and Hollie felt a delicious shiver of anticipation. 'But only when you're asleep. So I'm going to take you up to bed right now, which means morning will come faster.'

'*Oh!*'

'Would you like Mamá to come, as well?'

'Yes, please.'

'Come on, then. *Vamos!*'

Mateo giggled as, going past stone walls now covered with artwork, they mounted the beautiful curving stone staircase to his room, which was just along the corridor from their own. Silk rugs lay scattered over the floors, the draughty windows had been fixed and hung with sumptuous drapes and the building was gloriously warm. In fact, Hollie never stopped marvelling how cosy the place felt after its costly refurbishment, which had started just over three years ago.

Work had begun on the neglected castle soon after she and Maximo had vowed their love and commitment to each other, when they'd married in Trescombe's small church, with its sweeping views of the sea. It had been a small and simple ceremony. Hollie had worn a long dress of fine white wool, with a hooded and feather-trimmed cape, to keep out the bitter winter winds. And although they had been well into January, and it hadn't been Christmastime, her bouquet had nonetheless contained sprays of mistletoe, holly and ivy. Maximo's friend Javier had been best man and the ancient church had been filled with the competing sounds of Spanish and English chatter—though the Spanish had undoubtedly been the louder of the two. It had been, everyone said, the most beautiful wedding.

And they had made their life here, in Devon. Maximo continued to run his empire from this rural base—though they kept apartments in New York and Madrid. But he hadn't forgotten his vow to serve the community of his newly adopted home. He had completely refurbished the rather tatty hotel where first they'd met and the resulting five-star establishment now came under the umbrella of the Diaz group and brought many tourists flocking to the small town which nestled between moorland and sea. It had put Trescombe firmly on the map, although the narrow and winding access roads ensured that it was never going to be *too* much on the map, as Maximo drily commented.

Once their son had reached a year, Hollie had opened her tea shop—though someone else ran it for her. She'd fished out her best recipes and helped with batch cooking whenever she got the opportunity. She'd had the jaunty café painted in ice-cream colours of pink and lemon and spearmint, there was mismatched bone china on the tables, the waitresses wore old-fashioned frilly aprons and people came from miles around to taste her featherlight scones.

Her thoughts dissolving, Hollie sighed with pleasure as she watched her husband tuck his lookalike son into bed before going through the various nighttime rituals they had evolved, including a very special one tonight, which involved the reading of Clement Clarke Moore's famous Christmas Eve poem. And when the story had finished, and Mateo had fallen sound asleep, Hollie and Maximo crept from the room and into the corridor outside.

There she turned to him, looping her arms around his neck—unable to resist the temptation to plant a kiss on his lips and then to linger there. A feeling of excitement was bubbling up inside her and it was making her heart beat fast. There was something she needed to tell him and she wanted to find the right time, but for now she just kissed him.

'Everything's *almost* ready, I think,' she whispered, drawing her mouth away from his. 'The stockings have been hung—and Javier's room is prepared. I'm sure he's going to cause something of a stir when he arrives in Trescombe tomorrow morning.'

'Like I did, you mean?' he teased.

'I doubt it. Javier's not quite as arrogant as you,' she advised primly.

He laughed as he curved the palm of his hand over her buttock. 'And don't you just *hate* that arrogance, *mia belleza*?'

'Maximo.' Her throat dried as his fingers continued on their inexorable journey. 'What do you think you're doing?'

'What does it look like I'm doing?' His voice was careless, his arms strong. 'I am picking up my beautiful wife to carry her into the bedroom, because I know that kind of macho thing turns her on, and once we get there I am taking her to bed, where I intend to ravish her.'

'But it's Christmas Eve! And we haven't—'

'Haven't what?' he questioned as he kicked open their bedroom door.

'Finished wrapping all the presents, or—'

'Shut up,' he said gently, laying her down on the luxurious red velvet cover she'd bought in homage to their first night there. 'And come here.'

He undressed her, slowly and reverently, and just before he entered her Hollie almost told him.

But passion was a strange and beautiful thing. It stopped you having coherent thoughts. It blotted out the world so that all you could see and feel was that person in your arms, and all you could hear were soft moans which gradually became more frantic. And then it was happening, just as it always happened, and she was pulsing around him and his powerful body tensed for one exquisite moment before, finally, he collapsed into her arms.

Her heart was thumping heavily, her head was lying on his shoulder and all Hollie wanted was to go to sleep, but there wasn't time. 'Maximo...' she murmured lazily.

'Mmm...?'

'I've got something to tell you.'

'I know you have.'

'It has nothing to do with wrapping presents.'

'I know that, too.'

She rolled over to look at him and his black eyes were crystalline, hard and very bright. 'What do you know?'

'That you're having my baby again.'

'Yes, I am,' she breathed, slumping back against the pillow. 'But how did you *guess*?'

Maximo smiled, for this was the easiest question he'd ever had to answer. He didn't even have to think about it. 'Because I love you and because I know you. I know the look in your eyes and the smile on your lips when you have a new life growing inside you. And both of them are there now. Or at least, they were until a couple of minutes ago. Hollie, *querida*—what's the matter?' He frowned and smoothed his finger along the line of her quivering lip. 'Why are you crying?'

'You obviously don't know me that well at all! I'm crying because I'm happy, of course!'

And Maximo laughed softly, a feeling of pure joy wrapping around his heart as he brought her soft body closer to his and kissed the top of her silken head.

He had once thought there was no such thing as a perfect moment, but he had been wrong. Because this—*this*—was the perfect moment. These days his life was filled with them.

'And you spread happiness wherever you go, *mia belleza*,' he said softly. 'Happy Christmas, my beautiful wife.'

* * * * *

WE HOPE YOU ENJOYED
THIS BOOK FROM

H HARLEQUIN

PRESENTS

Escape to exotic locations where passion knows no bounds.

Welcome to the glamorous lives of royals and billionaires, where passion knows no bounds. Be swept into a world of luxury, wealth and exotic locations.

8 NEW BOOKS AVAILABLE EVERY MONTH!

COMING NEXT MONTH FROM

HARLEQUIN
PRESENTS

Available December 29, 2020

#3873 THE COST OF CLAIMING HIS HEIR
The Delgado Inheritance
by Michelle Smart
Blindsided by a shocking family secret, Emiliano Delgado spends one wildly passionate night with fiery Becky Aldridge. But as he's cursing himself for breaching his boundaries, Becky has life-changing news...

#3874 WHAT THE GREEK'S WIFE NEEDS
by Dani Collins
Tanja's whirlwind marriage to billionaire Leon Patrakis has been over since he returned to Greece five years ago... Yet, to keep the baby she's adopting, Tanja has a last request: they stay wed...in name only!

#3875 THE SECRETS SHE MUST TELL
Lost Sons of Argentina
by Lucy King
Finn Calvert is reeling from the shocking revelation that he has a son with lawyer Georgie Wallace! He's determined to step up as a father but as their chemistry reignites, he learns there are more secrets to be unveiled...

#3876 CHOSEN FOR HIS DESERT THRONE
by Caitlin Crews
Sheikh Tarek's kingdom needs a queen. And discovering a beautiful prisoner in his palace only puts the nation closer to the brink of collapse. Until he realizes Dr. Anya Turner might just be the key he's looking for...

HPCNMRA1220

#3877 THE KING'S BRIDE BY ARRANGEMENT
Sovereigns and Scandals
by Annie West

The long-standing betrothal of Princess Eva and King Paul is a political match. He's ready to release her from their promise, until an explosive kiss has him questioning everything he thought he knew about his royal bride!

#3878 THE COMMANDING ITALIAN'S CHALLENGE
by Maya Blake

By-the-book Maceo has fought to protect his company. He won't let free-spirited Faye upend his entire world by claiming it as her inheritance, without proving herself worthy. His challenge? Resisting their chemistry!

#3879 BREAKING THE PLAYBOY'S RULES
Wanted: A Billionaire
by Melanie Milburne

Millie tried to deny the sizzling chemistry with outrageously attractive Hunter before. The pain of her last relationship has made her wary. But when he breaks all his rules to whisk her off to Greece, she can't help that he makes her heart race...

#3880 HOW TO UNDO THE PROUD BILLIONAIRE
South Africa's Scandalous Billionaires
by Joss Wood

Hosting South Africa's wedding of the year is Radd Tempest-Vane's ticket to restoring his family's empire. As long as he finds a new florist, fast! Brinley Riddell is the perfect candidate...but an immediate, dangerous distraction!

YOU CAN FIND MORE INFORMATION ON UPCOMING HARLEQUIN TITLES, FREE EXCERPTS AND MORE AT HARLEQUIN.COM.

HPCNMRB1220

"How was the party?"

Becky had to untie her tongue to speak. "Okay. Everyone looked like they were having fun."

"But not you?"

"No." She sank down onto the wooden step to take the weight off her weary legs and rested her back against a pillar.

"Why not?"

"Because I'm a day late."

She heard him suck in a breath. "Is that normal for you?"

"No." Panic and excitement swelled sharply in equal measure as they did every time she allowed herself to read the signs that were all there. Tender breasts. Fatigue. The ripple of nausea she'd experienced that morning when she'd passed Paula's husband outside and caught a whiff of his cigarette smoke. Excitement that she could have a child growing inside her. Panic at what this meant.

Scared she was going to cry, she scrambled back to her feet. "Let's give it another couple of days. If it hasn't come by then, I'll take a test."

She would have gone inside if Emiliano hadn't leaned forward and gently taken hold of her wrist. "Sit with me."

Opening her mouth to tell him she needed sleep, she stared into his eyes and found herself temporarily mute.

For the first time since they'd conceived—and in her heart she was now certain they had conceived—there was no antipathy in his stare, just a steadfastness that lightened the weight on her shoulders.

Gingerly, she sat beside him, but there was no hope of keeping a distance for Emiliano put his beer bottle down and hooked an arm around her waist to draw her to him.

Much as she wanted to resist, she leaned into him and rested her cheek on his chest.

"Don't be afraid, *bomboncita*," he murmured into the top of her head. "We will get through this together."

Nothing more was said for the longest time and for that she was grateful. Closing her eyes, she was able to take comfort from the strength of his heartbeat against her ear and his hands stroking her back and hair so tenderly. There was something so very solid and real about him, an energy always zipping beneath his skin even in moments of stillness.

He dragged a thumb over her cheek and then rested it under her chin to tilt her face to his. Then, slowly, his face lowered and his lips caught hers in a kiss so tender that the little of her not already melting to be held in his arms turned to fondue.

Feeling as if she'd slipped into a dream, Becky moved her mouth in time with his, a deepening caress that sang to her senses as she inhaled the scent of his breath and the muskiness of his skin. Her fingers tiptoed up his chest, then flattened against his neck. The pulse at the base thumped against the palm of her hand.

But even as every crevice in her body thrilled, a part of her brain refused to switch off, and it was with huge reluctance that she broke the kiss and gently pulled away from him.

"Not a good idea," she said shakily as her body howled in protest.

Emiliano gave a look of such sensuality her pelvis pulsed. "Why?"

Fearing he would reach for her again, she shifted to the other side of the swing chair and patted the space beside her for the dogs to jump up and act as a barrier between them. They failed to oblige. "Aren't we in a big enough mess?"

Eyes not leaving her face, he picked up his beer and took a long drink. "That depends on how you look at it. To me, the likelihood that you're pregnant makes things simple. I want you. You want me. Why fight it anymore when we're going to be bound together?"

Don't miss
The Cost of Claiming His Heir,
*available January 2021 wherever
Harlequin Presents books and ebooks are sold.*

Harlequin.com

HPEXP1220